TOO MUCH TO LOVE

TRESSIE LOCKWOOD

CHAPTER 1

*C*rash!

Keleeja stabbed herself in the cheek with the electric toothbrush. Toothpaste dotted her mirror. Dang it. She'd just cleaned the thing yesterday. What in the world was that noise?

She opened the bathroom door and listened. "Ma, what was that?"

No answer.

Glass shifted somewhere in the house, and she went to investigate. Images of her mom having slipped and fallen ran through her head. Not that her mom was old enough that if she fell she couldn't get up.

"Ma?" Keleeja crossed the hall to her mom's room and opened the door. The place was strangely empty and quiet. Her mom had made her bed for once, and clothes weren't spilling out of the dresser and closet. Wow, Keleeja was impressed. Sometimes she felt like the parent and her mom the daughter with how irresponsible her mom tended to be.

Next, she tried the kids' room. All clear there too, but sheets hung half off unmade beds, and the pink and green butterfly carpet was littered with toys. She headed to the stairs. Where were they? Keleeja hoped they weren't getting into something while her mom's back was turned.

Now she spotted it, as she descended the stairs. Someone had knocked the lamp that sat on the hall table onto the floor, and the base shattered, not to mention the bulb. Even before she reached the bottom of the stairs, Tawney appeared and tried to gather the broken glass into a dish towel.

"Freeze," Keleeja ordered. "What do you think you're doing, Tawn?"

The four-year-old turned big brown eyes to Keleeja. On cue, they filled with tears. "I didn't do it. Lara did."

Keleeja sighed. "Stop crying and stand still before you cut yourself. Let me get you out of there. Where's Ma?"

"Gone."

Keleeja's stomach did a somersault. She decided Tawney didn't know what she was asking. Or *she* misunderstood *Tawney*. There was no way her mom would just be gone. Now that she was downstairs, Keleeja heard the girls in the kitchen, laughing and playing. A spoon clinked against a bowl, and a chair scraped across the floor.

Keleeja lifted Tawney up and deposited her safely out of reach of the glass. "In the kitchen," Keleeja told her. Tawney scampered off, and Keleeja used the broom and dustpan to sweep up the mess. This was her usual routine, not much time for brushing her teeth alone. Instead, she put out fires and tried to motivate her mom to take more of an interest.

Keleeja expected to find her mom in the kitchen. Lola stood on a chair at the stove, reaching toward one of the knobs. Lily held a bowl of lumpy pancake batter behind her sister. And Lara sat at the table, trying to clean up the batter-making mess. There was no sign of Keleeja's mom.

"Lola! Don't you touch that stove. You know better."

Lola frowned at her. "We want pancakes."

"And you thought you were going to cook them yourself? Get down."

Lara started to cry, which set off Lily. Lola's bottom lip quivered, but she didn't cry. She jumped off the chair.

Keleeja groaned. "If you girls clean this mess up, I'll make the pancakes. But I don't know if I'll have strength if I have to listen whining and crying at the same time.

Their little mouths snapped closed, and they sniffed while scrubbing their faces. Keleeja bit back a smile. She proceeded to clean up the mess herself and remake the batter. After she had all four of them settled at the table, eating their breakfast, she searched the house.

She passed from room to room, but she already knew the truth. Her mom was gone. By the time she went back upstairs to look inside her mom's closet, she knew what she would find. All her mom's clothes were gone. It was the one time her mom cleaned up after herself.

Keleeja sank onto the bed and pressed a hand over her mouth. Tears ran down her cheeks, and she shuddered with suppressed emotions. Tawney ran into the room and dove into her arms.

"Lee, you can't cry. You tell us to stop crying all the time."

Keleeja swallowed the lump in her throat and hugged the little girl. "That's because y'all cry at every little thing."

"I don't. I'm practically grown now."

"Didn't you cry earlier over the lamp?"

"That doesn't count."

"I don't know why not."

"It just doesn't." Tawney wiggled out of her arms and ran to look into the master bathroom. "When is Mama coming back? I want to go to the park. Plus, she said we could go to the dollar store and get a toy or some candy."

"I'm not sure, baby." Keleeja almost started crying again. "I'll have to call her."

"I'll do it!"

"No. You go get some clothes on. Did you brush your teeth?"

"Yes."

"No you didn't. Go do it, and help the girls too, please. I'll be in to check on you in a minute."

Tawney skipped out of the room. Keleeja went to grab her phone. She dialed her mom and waited. No answer. She dialed again, ten times in a row. At last the line connected.

"Um, Lee." Her mom's voice shook.

"Where are you, Ma? Better yet, why aren't you here?"

"I...I..." She heaved a sighed. "I need some time, Lee. Everything has become too much, and I just need some time off."

"You don't get time off from motherhood!"

"Easy, lower your voice. The girls will hear you. Are they awake?"

"You'd know if you were here. I can't believe you've done this. I can't believe you would run off, talking about you need a break. I should be the one running off. These are your kids! *Yours!* I didn't even get the chance to have kids of my own. You filled the house yourself, and you're talking about needing a break? You've got to be kidding me!"

Censor replaced the guilt in her mom's voice. "Keleeja Sampson, don't forget who you're talking to."

"Don't *you* forget who you are! You're the mother of five daughters—four of which are under five-years-old!"

"I'm sorry."

"Ma—"

The line disconnected. Keleeja stood there, shocked out of her mind. Her mom had just hung up on her, after abandoning her kids. Keleeja didn't know what to do or think and wondered how in the world they would be okay.

CHAPTER 2

*S*ix months later...

Keleeja checked her hair one last time in the mirror. She groaned. "Maybe I shouldn't go. Tawney is—"

"You're going." Her best friend, Autumn, turned Keleeja's shoulders and gave her a push toward her bedroom door. Keleeja sighed and descended to the first floor with Autumn behind her.

Autumn peeked outside and shook her head. "Not here yet. So tell me more about this guy. You said you met him at the coffee shop downtown. Is he cute?"

"He's okay." Keleeja sat down on the entry bench beside the front door and checked the inside of one of her heels. The shoe didn't feel quite right on her foot, and she worried about her feet hurting later during the date. "He looked good in his suit."

Autumn grinned. "What does he do?"

"I forgot."

"Lee!"

"I did. I was so nervous talking to him, and I'm even more nervous right now. What in the world do I think I'm doing going out tonight? Tawney's fever—"

"Has gone down, and all she was doing anyway was staying in bed watching cartoons. What would you do if you stayed home? Watch them with her?"

"I'd at least be able to keep my eye on her to make sure she's getting better."

"She is getting better, and I'll be the one keeping an eye on her. Lee, you deserve this break, unlike that person who calls herself your mother."

Keleeja laughed. "She calls herself my mom because she is."

"Have you heard from her in the last six months?"

"No. I don't know where she is. She hasn't called, and her cell phone has been disconnected." Keleeja got up to check the hall mirror. Her hair, which she'd pinned up, looked fine, and her makeup wasn't too bad. She didn't wear it all that often, so she was out of practice with the eye liner. It could have been better.

"I can't believe her. I wish she was here so I could tell her what I think of her. Anyway, you have me. I'm not going anywhere." Autumn appeared in the mirror behind her and squeezed Keleeja in a friendly hug.

Autumn was short and round with long chestnut hair that reached her butt. The girls loved playing in Autumn's hair, and she didn't mind letting them. Autumn might be single like Keleeja, but she had her own life, and Keleeja wouldn't drag her down with responsibilities that belonged to Keleeja's mom.

"I appreciate you with all my heart, Autumn. You

know that, but I'm not going to lean on you more than I have to. Tonight is rare, and well, I was feeling way too tempted with this dude's charm. He might not be all he seemed to be."

"You're *going* to find out."

"Jeez, you're bossy for someone so short." Keleeja teased her all the time about their height difference, Keleeja being five foot eight, and Autumn being five feet even.

"I resemble that remark." Autumn checked outside again. "Oh wow, you won't believe this."

"What?"

"He's either got money, or he's trying to impress you."

"What do you mean?"

"A limo."

"*What?*" Keleeja squeaked. "It's a first date, not an anniversary. Why in the world would he come in a limo?"

"Maybe he's rich. Oh, that could work, couldn't it?"

"No." Keleeja fought an urge to tell Autumn to send him away and run back to her room. "Number one, I don't know what I'll say about the girls. Men run off if a woman has one kid. I've got four."

"They're not from your body."

"Regardless."

"How does that make it bad that he has money?"

"Because men with money have choices, Autumn. They don't choose to date a woman with four mouths to feed, even if they can afford to feed them. Not that we're starving. We're doing fine."

"You were born good at budgeting. I wish it would rub off on me. Wait a minute. Why isn't he coming to the door? He better not blow the horn and expect you to come running out. He needs to come to the door like a gentleman to pick up a lady."

Keleeja snorted. "Okay, Grandma. Settle down."

The bell rang, and they looked at each other. Keleeja's butterflies multiplied, and she swallowed hard.

"Breathe," Autumn whispered. "It'll be fine. Tell yourself this date doesn't matter. He doesn't matter. You're just out to have a good time for a few hours. No biggie."

"You're right. Thanks, Autumn."

"You're welcome. And don't worry about Tawney. I'll keep you updated with texts and pics."

A few minutes later, Keleeja tipped out to the curb and slid into the back of the limo. The tall, silent man in the dark suit held the door open for her and dipped his head. "Good evening, ma'am."

In the dull light from the streetlamp, she caught a glimpse of the most handsome man she'd ever seen in her life. A strong smooth jawline, perfectly formed lips, and serious but kind eyes. He wore a chauffeur's hat, so she couldn't see his hair, but just that brief encounter left an impact. He had presence that didn't go with being a simple driver.

Get your head off the chauffeur, Keleeja. You have a date.

She slid across the seat to allow her date to climb in after her. "Marcus, this is a bit much. Do you always take your dates out in a limo?"

He smiled. "You don't like it?"

"I didn't say that, but…"

"I'm not showing off. I promise."

She gave him a doubtful look as the driver started the car. With no glass between the passengers in the back and the man up front, he could hear everything they said. Not that Keleeja minded. He didn't know her, and she didn't know him.

"Can I be honest?" her date asked.

"Please."

"I've been watching you for a while, at the coffee shop."

She widened her eyes.

He laughed. "Stalker, right? No. Seriously, I thought you were beautiful, but I wasn't sure about asking you out. Then there was this one time you were looking like wow, dressed to take charge in a gray skirt suit and these heels that made your legs look—uh, I mean—anyway you got a run in your pantyhose."

She didn't know what to think at this point in the story. Should she be flattered? Freaked out? Demand he stop the car and go back home? It sounded like he'd been watching her closely. Why hadn't she noticed?

"…and you just took it in stride when you saw the run. You got your coffee and walked out of that shop with the same confidence you walked into it with." He sounded impressed. "I thought, this one is beautiful and down to earth. I like that. So—eventually—I asked you out."

Keleeja covered her face, laughing. "Oh wow, I can't

believe you were impressed with that. It's not what you think. But… I guess, in some respects I would carry myself in the same way no matter what I wear."

He looked expectant, like he was interested in what she thought. Her attraction to him climbed higher as well.

"I'm not sure when I started thinking I have worth. I don't mean that in an arrogant way. I just mean I'm a person, you know? Just like everybody else. Why should I feel like I'm less than? In the case of the pantyhose, I probably had so much on my mind that day the run was the least of my issues."

"You remember which day I'm talking about?"

"No, sorry. I just know any given day, it doesn't stop." She wasn't ready to tell him about the girls. So far, they were off to a good start, and they hadn't arrived at the restaurant yet. She was getting a couple hours out of the house with a man and a fancy dinner. If the balloon of his admiration was going to pop, it could wait a while.

"Keleeja, you're something. Smart, beautiful, I want to know everything." He kissed her hand.

"Thanks." The suspicion that he was still trying to impress her wouldn't let go. She hoped he didn't blow money he couldn't afford on this date.

A little while later, they arrived at the restaurant, and Marcus helped her out of the limo. He turned to the driver. "Daniel, I'll ring you when we're ready, okay?"

"Yes, sir. Let me get the door for you." The driver's

smooth masculine voice danced along Keleeja's nerve endings, and she took one last look into his handsome face before she followed her date into the restaurant.

CHAPTER 3

"Marcus, are you okay?"

Keleeja studied him closely. His smile froze into place, but his gaze darted about like a caged animal. She imagined he searched his mind for an excuse to get out of there. The least she could have done was tell him about the girls *after* he took her home—like over text or something.

She bit back a groan. His reaction shouldn't surprise her. In fact, she was shocked he still sat there. They'd finished their meal, talked for the last hour and a half about everything from work to hobbies. He seemed like he was becoming a friend with the potential for more.

And that's why I let my guard down and told him about the girls. Stupid!

"Did you hear me?" she asked. "Tawney and the triplets are—"

He frowned. "Either you're lying as an excuse to get out of here, or you're a dirty ho."

"Excuse me?"

"Four kids?"

"I—"

"You look like you've never been pregnant with that body. It's tight and sexy, but maybe you're lying. Because I'm not good enough?"

She couldn't form words to respond. The acid dripping from his tongue, the anger burning in his eyes, it didn't seem like the man she'd been getting to know tonight was the same one sitting across from her now. He went from day to night in a flash. She didn't have the chance to tell him the girls were her sisters, not her own kids. But what did it matter with his attitude?

"You said you're twenty-seven, and you already have four kids. How many daddies? Four?"

She scraped her chair back and stood. "Goodnight, Marcus. This date was a mistake."

"Wait a minute." He waved for the waitress. "I'm going to pay for dinner and take you home. Don't let it be said I'm not a gentleman."

"So calling me a 'ho' is gentlemanly. Got it."

"You can't blame me for being mad."

"I can, and I do. Don't bother seeing me home. I can't stomach another second in your presence. And the next time you see me in the coffee shop, look the other way."

She left the restaurant and started walking down the street. Anger simmered in her veins, and hurt feelings drew a lump to her throat. She swallowed a few times, trying to get hold of her emotions.

The streetlight above her winked out, and she stumbled. A twist of her ankle reminded her that the one shoe rubbed. She wouldn't make it far wherever she was headed, and this wasn't a bus route. She would have to go back to the restaurant and call a taxi from there.

"Dang! I hope he's gone."

Just as she walked up to the front of the restaurant, the limo rolled to a stop in front of Marcus. She waited for him to get in, and when the limo pulled off, she shuffled into the light. No since going inside. She didn't want to talk to anyone, and the hostess was sure to ask if she needed help.

Her cell phone rang, and she groaned for the millionth time. "Autumn, hey."

"I'm so sorry for interrupting your date, Keleeja. Since you're still out, I assume it's going fine, but—"

"But what? Tell me, Autumn. Is Tawney okay?"

Worry tinged her friend's voice. "No. Her temperature is up again. I gave her the meds you left, but it's not working. She's shaky and complaining that she's cold. I think we should take her to the hospital."

"Oh God. I'm on my way. No, I'll meet you at the hospital. Take her to Mercy. I like their emergency room better. And bring the other girls too. Shoot, they're in bed, aren't they? Put some ice in a pillowcase and put it under Tawney's arms. I'll come home and take her to the hospital, if you don't mind staying longer with the others?"

"Of course. I'm here as long as you need me."

Keleeja got off the phone. Tears welled in her eyes, and she blinked them away so she could see her phone enough to dial for a taxi. If she'd come to the restaurant in her own car, she wouldn't be in this mess.

No, if I had sense enough to realize I'm never going to find a man with four babies to raise, I wouldn't be in this mess!

"Hello, yes, I need a taxi at—"

The limo slid to a halt in front of her, and the chauffeur climbed out to come around and wrench the back door open. "Get in."

She leaned forward to find Marcus huddled in the back. His scowl said he didn't agree with coming back for her. She straightened. "He doesn't want to take me home."

"Regardless. He brought you here. He needs to take you home. A man doesn't leave a woman alone at night, period. Get in. *Please.*"

A desperate need to get to Tawney made her toss aside her pride and get in. As soon as they arrived at her house, she jumped out of the limo and ran up the drive. Autumn must have been watching for their arrival because she was already coming out the door, carrying Tawney.

Keleeja unlocked her car and settled her little sister into the back.

"Lee, I don't feel good."

"I know, baby. Big Sis is here. You're going to be okay. Promise. Autumn, I'll call you."

Keleeja jammed her key into the ignition and

turned. Nothing. Her car was dead. Shock and confusion hit. She twisted the key over and over and stabbed the gas pedal with her foot. Nothing more than a *click, click, click* met her ears.

"This can't be happening." She started to cry now because Autumn's car was in the shop. Keleeja and the girls had picked up Autumn earlier in the evening to bring her over to the house to babysit. And Keleeja shouldn't be surprised that the car battery was dead. Lara forgot to shut the car door daily. With the overhead light on, Keleeja's battery was always going dead after a few hours.

She looked through the windshield to find that the limo hadn't pulled away after she jumped out of it. In fact, the chauffeur was headed up her drive at that moment.

"Can you give me a jump, please?" she begged. "My little sister is sick. I have to take her to the hospital. I know you're on a job, but—"

"Come on. I'll drive you."

"No, a jump is fine. My car isn't broken down. It's just the battery. Lara can be scatterbrained and…" Why was she explaining all the unnecessary details? She worried about Tawney.

"I'll drop you at the hospital and then come back to pick you up. It will take less time than hoping your problem is only your battery. Don't worry. My boss is very understanding."

She decided not to argue and followed him, clutching Tawney in her arms. Soon she was hurrying into the emergency room, having mumbled a thank you over her shoulder. She promised herself later she would let him know how grateful she was from the bottom of her heart. What was his name?

Daniel.

He'd been her unexpected knight in shining armor.

CHAPTER 4

Six months ago...

"Isabella," Daniel growled. "What is this?"

He held up the package of little pink pills. Even as he asked, he knew what it was, and the knowledge choked him in anger. His wife flushed. Her mouth flapped open and closed, and she stuttered, probably thinking up another lie.

"I'm...keeping them for...I mean..." She huffed. "Look the fact is, I wasn't ready to have a kid, Danny. And now I am. Those are old. You don't have to worry about them."

"How long?"

She widened eyes he used to drown in with love. Now all he saw was deceit. He'd thought her tiny stature and delicate appearance was a perfect match to his protective nature. It was all an illusion. Isabella had been manipulating him, using her femininity from the start. Really, he shouldn't be angry at her as much as himself, for letting her outward appearance sway him.

"How long what?" She tried to sound innocent, but he heard deception.

"We talked about having kids right after we were married. That was ten years ago. So explain to me how long it's been since you were 'ready'—even though you said you were back then."

"I don't appreciate this third degree, Danny. I'm your wife, not some woman on the street."

"How long!"

"I was never ready, okay? I work hard for this body, and I didn't want it messed up by getting fat. Plus, kids take up a lot of time, and… Like I said, I'm ready *now*. Doesn't that count for something?"

His cell phone rang. It was Colin.

"Hello?"

"I'll get straight to the point, buddy."

Daniel's stomach dropped.

"You were right. She's got a guy on the side. From what I could find out, it's been going on for about three months."

"Thanks."

"Do you want me to dig further? I can run a check on him."

"No, it's fine. Thanks for your help."

"Any time. Why don't you meet me for a drink later, and we can talk about what you're going to do?"

"There's nothing to discuss." Daniel watched Isabella squirm as he stared at her while he spoke on the phone. She'd always had a sixth sense of what was coming. There wasn't a doubt in his mind she knew *he* knew about the affair.

"Danny." She widened those baby blues, perfectly made up, and laid a hand on his arm. As she stepped closer to him, he caught a whiff of her perfume, the one he had purchased for her birthday. The scent would forever remind him of her, but right then it choked him. All he could think about was someone else touching her when she'd belonged to him.

No, she was never mine. Not really. I was the fool.

"Talk to you later, Colin." He disconnected the call and stuffed his phone into his pocket.

"Danny, I wanted to talk to you about something."

"Save it."

She gasped. "You've never talked to me like that before."

He gritted his teeth, resenting the hurt tone. She kept trying to manipulate him. As he stared at her, he saw the shift, when she dropped the act.

"I'm leaving," she said simply.

He thought he prepared for this confrontation. It had been coming for a couple weeks after he suspected what she was up to and asked Colin for help. Regardless, it cut him to his core. He dreamed of having his own family, what he never had growing up.

"It's not that I don't love you, Danny, but we've grown apart and..."

"Stop." He headed out of the bedroom. "I don't want to hear your excuses. Just do whatever it is you're going to do."

"Danny! Come back here. I'm talking to you. *Danny!*"

~

PRESENT DAY...

Daniel resettled in his seat and tipped his hat over his eyes. He was tired. It had been a long night, and he wanted his bed. Instead, he drove back to the hospital and found a place to park the limo to wait. Seeing that woman's face so full of fear, and her holding the small child in her arms, struck him hard. Even if he went home, he wouldn't sleep well. Not with that on his mind.

Wait, he didn't get her name. Before he walked away, he gave her one of his cards. She had his number. When she needed him, she would call. Then there was the chance the hospital would keep the child. She might stay the night there as well.

"If she's anything like Isabella, she'll let someone else take the responsibility while she does what she wants."

He sighed. No, he wouldn't think of his failed marriage. Not now that he signed the divorce papers. He hadn't seen Isabella in months, and then the papers arrived. All the emotions he thought he settled resurfaced. But it was done now. He was a free man.

"Not what I wanted to be."

The mystery woman came back to mind. He recalled his first sight of her, slender, shapely, an African American beauty if ever he saw one. When she looked into his face as he'd held the door for her, he saw the startled reaction. He got that a lot. Women found him attractive. So what? Looks meant nothing.

He chuckled under his breath. "Now you know. But not at twenty-three when you fell hard for a pair of sexy legs and a pouty mouth. Stupid!"

He chided himself for thinking again about Isabella and decided to speculate more on the mystery woman. What kind of person goes out on a date with a sick child at home? She said the little girl was her sister, but it was probably a lie. She didn't have to lie to him. He didn't need to be impressed with her.

"Stop, Daniel. Don't let them make you bitter. It's not worth it."

He must have dozed because the next thing he knew his phone was ringing. The dash clock read two a.m.

"Hello?"

"I'm so sorry to call this late. I should have called a taxi, but—" He liked her husky tone.

"Don't worry about it. Are you staying at the hospital or do you need me to come get you?"

"I have to get home to the other girls."

That shocked him. "Other girls?"

"Yes, never mind. They aren't keeping Tawney. Her temperature's down, and she seems to be doing fine. The doctor thinks she has a virus, and—you're not interested in the details. Um, can you take us home, please?"

"Yes, I'll be at the entrance in thirty seconds."

"Thirty seconds?"

He disconnected the call and started the car. When he pulled up to the emergency entrance, she stood there swaying a bit, holding the little girl in her arms.

He jumped out of the car to sweep the small bundle away from her.

She started to protest, but he cut her off. "Open the door, and get in. I'll hand her in to you."

"Thanks."

They were soon on the road, and he kept the partition lowered so he could speak to her. "I'm sorry, I didn't get your name."

She'd been nodding before he spoke, her chin bumping her chest over and over. A small hand covered a big yawn. "Keleeja Sampson. Thanks so much for your help, Daniel."

He almost forgot that she knew his name from his business card.

"You said your boss is understanding, but the limo company is called *Morgan Limousine Service*. Your last name is Morgan. You're the boss."

"Guilty."

Her home wasn't too far from the hospital, and with no traffic on the road, they made it there in record time.

"I'll carry her in. You unlock the door."

She huffed. "You're pretty bossy. If I wasn't so sleepy, I'd tell you what I think of that attitude."

He grinned. "Not bossy. Efficient. Plus, you're wobbling and limping. I don't want you to drop Tawney."

She startled when he used the little girl's name and then seemed to recall she'd said it to him over the phone. When she opened the front door, light and shouts from several voices greeted them.

"What are you girls doing up?" Keleeja demanded. "Autumn, why aren't they in bed? And Lola, an apple at this time of night, really?"

The woman Keleeja had called Autumn gave her an apologetic look. "I'm sorry, Lee. They woke up and figured out that you and Tawney weren't home. They were so worried, they wouldn't go back to sleep. I was worried too, so here we are. How's Tawney, and who is this?"

Daniel gaped at the scene before him. Three additional girls stood there in the hall, all smaller than Tawney. Caramel-colored skin, every one of them little beauties with curiosity-filled hazel eyes. The second he stepped into the house with Keleeja, one of the girls burst into tears and threw herself at Keleeja's legs. That seemed to trigger the water works from the other three, and soon the cacophony escalated. Everyone clamored for Keleeja's attention and to see for themselves that Tawney wasn't dead.

How would kids this age even know about death?

Looking into their little faces with tears wetting their cheeks and the fronts of their pink frilly night dresses, confusion hit Daniel. He scrambled to think of some way to calm them down. Normally, in tight situations, he was level-headed and logical, but this was new. He felt like he'd crossed into enemy territory without a clue to what he was supposed to be doing. And yet, he longed to comfort the girls.

"Calm down," Keleeja ordered as she kicked her shoes off. "Tawney's fine. Everything is fine. Stop crying."

The sobs turned instantly into sniffles. Daniel gaped.

The little one Keleeja called Lola tugged on Daniel's pants leg. He was pretty sure her fingers were coated with apple juice. "Let me see."

Keleeja rushed to apologize, but he got down on one knee and let Lola see Tawney sleeping peacefully in his arms. How she could have rested in the middle of all the noise, he didn't know.

"I'm sorry. Let me take her, Daniel. Thank you so much for bringing us home. It's late. Um, how much do I owe you?"

He blinked at her as she took the child from his arms. His mind took its time clearing. He was starting to wonder if this was why his client earlier had wanted to abandon her. She had four daughters, all under six, if he had to guess. Insane.

"Lee, who is he?" Lola stared up at him, still handsy.

They called their mom by her nickname? No, wait, she'd said Tawney was her sister. Were the others her sisters too? Surely not. A woman with a daughter that was—late twenties?—wouldn't have three more kids.

"Mind your business, little miss, and keep your sticky hands to yourself. Ugh, I'm sorry, Daniel. How much?"

"Nothing. My bill was paid for the evening."

She gasped. "He…never mind. I don't want to think about that. Thanks again. Good night."

He nodded and started for the door, but so many questions ran through his head. Curiosity about her and the girls. Was there a husband? No, she'd gone out on a date earlier. Of course, it didn't mean she wasn't cheating, but he doubted she'd have her date come to the house in such a flashy way if that were the case.

At the door, he turned back, reluctant to go despite exhaustion. "I hope Tawney will be okay."

"She will. I'm sure." Keleeja smiled at him.

For a moment, something stirred inside. He stuffed it down. Looks meant nothing. Rather he wouldn't *allow* them to mean anything. She was beautiful. He could acknowledge that. She had a big family. He hoped she could appreciate it.

"You have my card. If you need my services, don't hesitate to call." He couldn't imagine a situation where she would need to, but he said it anyway and left.

A sliver of regret washed over him as he figured he wouldn't see her or the little girls again.

CHAPTER 5

"I'm doing it."

Daniel looked over at Colin. "You're...?"

His friend set a ring box on the table and ran a hand over his head. "I'm going to ask her to marry me."

"Whoa. Congratulations. You're a brave man."

Colin grinned. "I'm thinking about asking Jerry to be my best man. What do you think?"

"Ah..."

Colin snorted. "It was a joke. You know you'll be my best man."

"I didn't want to assume."

"Liar." Colin teased him.

They had been friends since high school, and there wasn't a man Daniel trusted more than Colin. Plus, he was pretty sure his friend felt the same way about him. It was Colin he had turned to when his marriage fell apart and his dreams went up in smoke.

"So when are you going to pop the question?" Daniel admitted to himself that he was a little jealous.

He'd met Sherrie and liked her. The three of them had hung out multiple times along with Isabella. Daniel recalled Isabella had behaved as if Colin's girl was a threat to her personally. It should have clued him in to her nature.

"It's got to be big and special."

"The proposal or the wedding?"

"We haven't gotten to the wedding yet. I'm talking about the proposal. I've been informed that it must be memorable." Colin sighed.

Daniel chuckled. "'Informed'? Well since she knows it's coming, can it really be everything you're saying?"

"You don't understand, buddy. I'm talking about her mom. She gave me instructions, and I must follow them to the letter or else."

"Wow, and you *want* to marry into that family?"

"It's great. Don't worry. My future mother-in-law is tough, but fair. And I like her okay. Could be worse." Colin shoveled the last bite of food into his mouth and pushed his plate away. "I love Sherrie. You know that."

"Yeah, I know."

"I didn't expect to meet a woman like her. She…"

"Completes you?"

Colin cringed and then laughed. "I guess I was getting sappy. Sorry."

"Don't sweat it. I understand. Once upon a time, I felt the same way about Isabella. I learned later that I was delusional."

"Don't. She's not worth thinking about even for a second."

"You're right."

"You'll meet the right one and have eight kids before you know it."

Daniel snorted. "Yeah, okay."

He too pushed his plate away, but he hadn't eaten more than half his food. His appetite wasn't what it normally was. Maybe he was coming down with something. The thought took him back to that incident with the little girl.

"Hey, Colin, you won't believe what happened the other night."

"What's that?"

Daniel told him about Keleeja and about Tawney and her sisters. "It was crazy. Four girls. Can you imagine?"

Colin looked at him for a second with a closed expression. "Was she cute?"

"Which one? Tawney? Lola? Sure. They were all adorable. Fresh-faced, sweet." Daniel sighed. "I imagine if I had a daughter, she would be that cute."

His heart ached with longing.

"I meant the *big* sis."

That startled Daniel. Colin concluded right away that the girls weren't Keleeja's. Maybe it was because Colin didn't have the experience of a lying cheating spouse. He had no reason to think that all women were hiding something.

Neither do you. Stop it!

Daniel shrugged. "She was beautiful, if you like that sort."

"So when will you see her again?"

"Who said I was going to? She was out on a date with a client. That's how I met her."

"And? You said it didn't go well."

"And nothing. I'm not in the market for another woman. And did you hear what I said? She's raising four little girls. That's an instant family."

"Your life goal is to have a family."

"You're exaggerating." Heat flooded Daniel's face.

The waitress arrived at the table and slid a note toward Colin. She leaned closer to him and whispered. "A secret admirer."

She winked and left them alone. Colin picked up the note to read. Neither he nor Daniel were surprised because everywhere Colin went, women were always coming on to him. It never failed.

Daniel studied his friend. Dark curls and silver eyes, he wasn't the dark and dangerous or mysterious type. Not with that clear straight-forward expression. Women stared at Daniel like they found him handsome, but they didn't approach him as often as they did Colin. Maybe it was the boy-next-door good looks that made him more accessible.

"This is one issue I expect to be resolved when I get married."

"You hope." Daniel doubted it. "Her number?"

Colin handed the note over. He didn't scan the restaurant to see if he could meet the woman's eyes. Instead, he picked up the ring box and played with it in plain sight. Daniel shook his head in amusement and read the note.

"I'd love to buy you a drink. Better yet, we could make the drink a follow-up... Call me."

"Wow, are you going to call her?" Daniel teased him. He knew Colin better than that.

"If I were single, I might. *Maybe*. I like to be the one doing the chasing. I know from experience the kind of woman I'm attracted to. She'll wait for me to make the first move. But I've already found her."

"I never thought to ask. Does Sherrie know you get this kind of attention?"

"She does." Colin flushed. "She thinks it's funny."

"They haven't done it with her there, have they?"

"No. But I told her about it. She wasn't even intimidated. That's how I know she's the one."

Daniel chuckled. "And yet, she has a forceful mom."

"Sherrie takes after her dad. He's great."

"Ah."

"So would you like me to look into this Keleeja for you?" Colin pulled out his phone, ready to take notes. "Unusual name. How's it spelled?"

"Absolutely not. I told you. It was special circumstances. There's no need to ever see her again. I don't have a clue how to spell that name. Just because you run a private investigations firm doesn't mean you have to investigate every person that comes within ten feet of me."

"How else can I appease my curious nature?"

"You mean nosy nature."

"I resemble that remark." Colin tapped away on his

phone. "Hey, what do you say we make the bachelor party a trip somewhere?"

"A trip?"

"Yeah, you need to get away, take your mind off things."

"I thought this was about you. And maybe your other buddies won't have the time in their schedule to get away. I've got bookings up to my ears."

"Yeah, and your drivers can take care of all of them. The wedding is about me, but I can't neglect making sure you get back on track."

"I wasn't aware I was off track."

Colin nodded toward his plate. "Think I hadn't noticed? I'm trained to take everything in, Daniel. You're off your feed, and you look paler than usual."

"Am I a horse?"

"Yes, and I'll ride you until you get it together. Grin and bear it."

Daniel laughed. "Fine. A trip. I can manage the company from anywhere—for a week."

"Good man."

Colin paused to answer his phone, and Daniel tried to finish his meal. He didn't like having his friend fuss over him like he was a kid. Besides, if Colin noticed his issues, it meant he needed to get a hold of himself. Isabella wasn't worth him losing his health.

"*What?*" Colin paled. He gripped his phone so tight it cracked under the pressure.

Daniel tensed.

"Which hospital?"

Daniel shoved his chair back and signaled for the

waiter. He was already settling the bill when Colin ended the call. His friend's voice came out strangled as he explained what happened.

"It's Sherrie. She's been in an accident."

Daniel clenched his jaw. "Let's go. I'll drive."

CHAPTER 6

"Let's go for ice cream," Keleeja suggested.

Autumn moaned but didn't move. She slumped over the dining room table, eyes closed, frowning. "What's the point? Nothing matters."

"It will make you feel better."

"How can it? I didn't get the promotion I deserved. Why? I'll tell you why. Because she's pretty, and I'm short and fat!"

"You know better."

Autumn sat up in a huff. "I'm the best graphic designer at that firm, and everybody knows it. I've been there seven years, and I am the best candidate for Creative Director, but who gets it? The conniving little suck-up with her cleavage all over the conference room table."

Keleeja laughed. "Cleavage on the table? That must be a sight."

"It's gross, but she shows it off because the men who

run the company like it. Maybe if I had shown mine off —and you can bet I've got more."

Keleeja agreed but not out loud. Autumn tried to downplay her plump figure more than show it off. She was far more conservative than Keleeja. Not that Keleeja was like the showy woman at her friend's job.

"You shouldn't have to sell your body for a promotion."

"Right!"

"Ice cream will make you feel better."

"Is that for me or you?"

"For the girls. But we can both benefit. That new shop down on Front Street has a delicious brandy banana caramel flavor. I tried it the other night in a waffle cone. I want some more. Let's go."

"Alright, but I warn you. I'm in a foul mood."

"I didn't notice."

A short while later, Keleeja followed her sisters into the ice cream shop. Autumn slugged in after her, but she perked up a little at the scent of caramel. The shop sold caramel apples and toffee popcorn, as well as ice cream.

"Maybe I'll get an apple," Autumn murmured. "That's healthy, right?"

"The fact that its dripping with hardened caramel probably cancels out any health benefits."

"I don't care. I'm having one."

"Lee, I want vanilla. *Lee!*"

Keleeja sighed. "Alright, Lara. You don't have to tell me at the top of your lungs. Are you sure you don't want something different? You always have vanilla at home, and you had vanilla the last time we were here."

The fairest of the triplets flushed in frustration. "Vanilla."

"Okay. I'm just asking. Not trying to convince you."

Keleeja listened to the shouted choices from her sisters. One second they wanted one flavor. Then they switched to something else. The girl behind the counter looked a bit frazzled, but Keleeja knew better than to order before the girls made up their minds.

"Just a sec. They'll know what they want soon. Please, go ahead and wait on someone else."

"Take your time." The woman tried to sound patient, but the slight bite in her tone told the truth. Plus her right eye twitched a little. Keleeja wondered how she survived working in an ice cream shop. This was a tourist area and guaranteed to have plenty of kids coming in with their parents.

The bell over the door dinged, and the associate looked up. Her lips parted, and a look of wonder came into her eyes. All hints of irritation disappeared. Keleeja looked around to see who brought on this metamorphosis. Maybe the woman's boyfriend or husband came to visit her at work.

When Keleeja's gaze met Daniel's, she imagined her reaction wasn't all that different than the server's. She schooled her features in a hurry. More shocking than seeing him again was the fact that it wasn't a trick of the street or moon lights that made her think he was the most handsome man she'd ever seen.

In daylight, his good looks were breathtaking—

especially the green eyes. That night, she'd seen friendliness in their depths but wasn't able to pinpoint the color. Now she saw them clearly. He drew closer, and she noticed something different. Sadness. Her heart twisted in sympathy.

He smiled. "Hello."

"Hello."

"Fancy meeting you here."

She laughed. "Not so much. There are plenty of hotels down here, and this is the best ice cream shop in town."

He scanned the shop with interest. "Is it? I've never stopped in. Usually when I'm downtown, I'm working. I'll take your word for it."

Today, instead of a black chauffeur's uniform, he had dressed in jeans and a t-shirt. He looked amazing regardless.

Autumn sidled over and stuck her hand out. The giant smile suggested her job slipped right out of her mind. "Hello again. I'm Autumn. We didn't get to meet officially last time. But you probably don't remember me."

He took her hand. "I remember. Autumn, nice to meet you. I'm Daniel. And these are…?"

He seemed genuinely interested in meeting the girls. They gathered around Keleeja, demanding she get on with the ice cream order. Keleeja noticed Lola wasn't with the group and turned to look for her.

Lola stood on tiptoe at the counter and pointed. "Two really big scoops of that one." Then as an afterthought, "Please."

Keleeja shook her head in amusement. "*One.* These little scamps are my sisters. The bold one over there is Lola. This is Lara, Lily, and you remember Tawney. Girls, this is Mr. Daniel. Tawney, say thank you. He's the one who took you to the hospital and brought us home."

Tawney's eyes rounded with nervousness. She slipped behind Keleeja, peeked out at Daniel, and whispered her thanks.

"Sorry. She's a little shy sometimes just like Lara. Lily not so much, and anyone from a mile away can see Lola doesn't have a shy bone in her body."

Daniel chuckled. "Hello, ladies. Nice to meet you. Keleeja, I don't want to stop you from ordering. They look like they're chomping at the bit to get ice cream. Is it good here, Tawney?"

"Very good," Tawney whispered. "The smores is the best."

"I'll keep that in mind. Thanks."

As they placed their orders, Keleeja felt his gaze on her. She tried to concentrate on taking care of the girls, but she kept wondering if he thought she lied that they were her sisters. He didn't know that if the girls heard her lie, they'd pipe up loud and clear with the truth. That's how little kids were. They were most honest when one wanted to be sneaky. Keleeja had found it funny and frustrating at various times.

Out on the street, the girls walked ahead of Keleeja, eating their ice cream, while Keleeja walked side-by-side with Daniel and Autumn. She noticed he bought the smores ice cream—to Tawney's delight. Keleeja doubted he did so to win Tawney over to get closer to her.

Yeah, right. The last guy that found out about them ran off. Get out of fantasy land.

"I promise, I'm not stalking you," Daniel said.

She laughed. "I didn't think that. Our downtown area is small. We were bound to run into each other at some point. Maybe we have before."

He agreed.

"And who would stalk me? For the overabundance of snotty noses and sticky fingers? I don't think so."

He laughed. "Your sisters are a sight to behold when they're worked up. That night... I didn't know what to think."

She should have known. "Yeah, the last guy wanted to leave me stranded."

He frowned. "He's not a man!"

She laughed. "I'm kidding. He offered to take me home at first. My pride wouldn't let me agree. I wasn't expecting much from that date anyway."

"Because you have your sisters. Is your...I don't want to intrude on your privacy."

"But you're curious."

Pink stained his cheeks. Her heart skipped a beat because she could imagine him as a little boy or how his son would look. So cute it was painful. A new thought struck her, and she looked down at his hand. No wedding ring but she had the feeling there was a slight impression there. The skin might be fairer in the middle of the tan around it, but it could be her imagination.

Stop looking, Keleeja. It doesn't matter.

"Well," she began. A sudden urge came over her to drive him away with the truth. It happened far too often, a protective mechanism.

Autumn darted forward to walk with the girls. "Lara, you're dripping everywhere, honey. Let me help you."

Keleeja knew what her friend was doing and appreciated it. She shouldn't get her hopes up though.

"My mom isn't around," Keleeja explained to Daniel.

His eyes widened. "You mean she's away on business?"

"No, like abandonment. I'm raising my sisters." She bit back the bitterness.

"I'm sorry. I should have kept my curiosity to myself. It was insensitive."

"No, it's fine. It's been six months or so. And really the only thing different is that I don't see her. I've been looking after them since they were born. They might as well be mine."

"You love them very much. I hear it in your voice and see it in your eyes."

"Of course. What's not to love? They're super cute and sweet. Even when they get on my last nerve, I adore them."

He smiled. "You're to be envied."

"Wow. No one's ever said that before." She studied his face. "But you mean it, don't you?"

"Why wouldn't I?"

"Because kids are a huge responsibility. Just one can

overwhelm most people. I've got four. Autumn helps me a ton, and I love her for it." She shrugged. "I don't have unrealistic expectations, and that's fine. If my life is all about them until they're eighteen or whatever, so be it."

"Hm."

She decided not to ask what that "hm" meant. Instead, she figured she could be nosy with him as he'd been with her. "You're married, right?"

His eyebrows rose. "Why do you say that?"

She pointed. "Your ring finger looks like you took off your ring. If you were hoping—"

He chuckled, holding up a hand in surrender. "I'm newly divorced. My finger hasn't recovered just yet from wearing a ring for the last ten years."

"Oh no. I'm sorry."

"Thank you. So am I." He sighed. "I thought it would be different."

"I hear that."

Was that the sadness she saw in his eyes? Most likely. He must have a broken heart, which meant he wasn't open to anything new. Not that she thought he was looking her way. His walking and chatting with them was his way of being friendly.

"I knew I saw sadness in your eyes that wasn't there the last time." She kicked herself for admitting it. Maybe the words slipped out because she was interested in his reaction to them. Really, she should send him on his way before she started getting notions.

A haunted look came into his eyes, shocking her to her core.

"I'm sorry." She was an idiot for pointing out his pain.

His jaw tightened, and he looked toward the girls. The faraway light in his gaze said he didn't see them. "I saw Isabella for what she was long before our separation and then divorce. The sadness is something else—that hit harder."

She waited.

"I'd rather not discuss it."

"I'm sorry. I—"

"Don't apologize. I poked my nose into your business. You had every right to reciprocate." His smile seemed much more forced. "What do you think of having dinner with me sometime?"

Her mouth fell open. "Dinner? Like a date?"

"Are you against dating? Or me?"

"Neither, but I mean…" What was she doing? A real live man asked her out—a guy who knew about the girls. Even if he did it on a whim or if he deluded himself into thinking he could handle dating a single mom of four, she could at least enjoy the free meal and the company.

Not to mention looking into those eyes for a few hours!

"Sure. Why not?"

He chuckled. "You make a guy feel wanted."

"I'm sorry. I didn't mean to sound like that."

"Again, don't apologize. Just be yourself, exactly the way you are. Friday?"

"I have to see if Autumn can—"

"Friday's great," Autumn shouted from several yards ahead of them.

"She's got supersonic hearing," Daniel mused.

Keleeja laughed. "She's sweet and very supportive. I guess we're on for Friday night. Still have my number?"

"I do."

He said his goodbyes and disappeared. Autumn ran over to her, bursting with excitement. "I knew it! The moment I saw him I knew he was going to be significant in your life."

"Autumn, don't get worked up. You saw what happened the last time."

"Nope. We're already miles ahead on that one. He's met the girls and likes them. He might be the one, Lee."

"He's definitely not the one. 'The One' doesn't exist for me. I'm learning to believe that every day."

"Hang on."

Autumn disappeared from the line, and Keleeja strained to hear what was said in the background. She could have sworn her friend said something about plotting revenge. Wasn't she calling from work? What in the world was she doing, and who was she talking to?

"I'm back. So what happened? I thought we were on for tonight. I bought several movies for me and the girls to watch tonight. I know they haven't seen these."

"Why are you buying movies? I pay good money to stream channels they can watch."

"It's more fun to pop in a DVD."

"How old are you?"

"Never mind that. What happened with your date tonight?"

"He came to his senses."

"Lee."

"He did. Twenty minutes ago, he called with some lame excuse. I can't say I blame him, but I'm mad. I was looking forward to it. I expected him to call and cancel all week. Then when I woke up this morning, I thought wow, it's going to happen. I should have waited a few hours."

"Aw, sweetie. Give me his number. I'm going to give him a call and tell him what I think of cowards. I'm feeling particularly friendly toward men right now."

"Meaning if you could get away with skinning one…"

"Give me his number."

"No, crazy. Just let it go. It's better now than later after a night of drowning in his eyes. Ugh, I'm not the romantic type. I'm the realistic type."

"You'd be romantic if life let you."

"Autumn, are you at work? What's going on down there?"

"I can't say."

"What?"

"It might get interesting come Monday."

"Don't get fired."

"I won't. But if I can't afford my rent one day…."

"You can live with us. We've got my mother's room available. None of the girls wanted to give up sleeping together in the same room."

"They will when they're older. Probably Tawney first, when she gets to *that* age."

"Ugh, don't remind me."

Keleeja was about to gripe some more about Daniel when her phone buzzed. She checked the display and was surprised to see his name flash on the screen. Too late, she should have blocked him. Temptation made her put Autumn on hold and answer.

She struggled for a couldn't-care-less tone. "Hello?"

"Keleeja, you haven't cancelled the babysitter yet, have you?"

"Why?"

He sounded hesitant. "I know what I'm going to suggest isn't right for a first date, but if I leave things the way they are, you'll block my calls."

"I wouldn't. You said you had something important come up."

"Hm."

"Alright fine. I *might* have." She laughed. He was different. She had to give him that.

"I'll pick you up at seven-thirty, but we'll have dinner at a friend's house tonight."

"Kind of late."

"I have a job first. Is it too late?"

"No, it's okay. You said a friend. Who?"

"His name is Colin. I'll explain everything when I pick you up."

"Are you coming in a limo?"

"No, I'll drive my personal car. Or were you spoiled from the other night and want a repeat?"

She laughed. "No, I'm trying to let my neighbors move on to other topics to gossip about."

"Okay, see you later."

Keleeja jumped back over to Autumn. "You still there?"

"I'm here. What's up?"

"Can you still watch the girls?"

"I knew it!"

Keleeja rolled her eyes toward the ceiling.

KELEEJA FOUND IT ODD THAT SHE WOULD GET TO SEE Daniel's friend's house before she saw his. Not that she expected them to get that far. She couldn't help *hoping*, but tonight was odd. They circumvented the norms, so she didn't know what to expect or how to feel.

On the drive over, Daniel explained the situation with his friend. "Colin was about to ask his girlfriend to marry him when she had a very serious accident."

"Oh no. I'm so sorry." Her heart ached for the man and woman she didn't know. Family meant so much, and it hurt to think someone suffered such loss even if she had never met them.

"Thanks. It's been very hard for him, and I don't know how to be there for him other than to just *be* there."

"That's all you can do sometimes. If he's grieving her loss, then surely it's not a good time for visitors, definitely not a date."

"Sherrie's not dead."

She gasped. "What?"

"She's alive and staying in a rehabilitation center. Colin spends most of his time with her during visiting hours. His entire focus has been on supporting her to get better."

"Then…"

"He's home tonight."

"Daniel, seriously, this isn't a good idea. I don't want to get in the way or complicate his life any more than it is." Part of her felt like Daniel was being selfish dragging her in the middle of something that must be an emotional struggle. What would she say to Colin? Were they supposed to laugh and shoot the breeze like he wasn't thinking about his fiancée?

"Please."

The one word stopped her protest, charged as it was with feelings she couldn't identify. She tried to see his face in the car's dark interior. He pressed his lips together, and although shadows stretched across the side of his face, she imagined he tensed his jaw.

The low squeak of his hands gripping the steering wheel made her look there. Daniel was suffering too. All of it convinced her she was right. This was the worst date ever—worse than her last one where the guy called her a ho. Daniel must be the most inconsiderate person or the densest that he couldn't see the mistake in inviting her to Colin's house. Regardless, she kept her mouth closed and went with him.

Colin lived in a modern farmhouse styled home, a new development from the looks of it. All the houses in Keleeja's neighborhood were older, from the nineteen seventies. Colin's place appeared to have been built in the last year or two.

Daniel stopped behind a black jaguar in the driveway. Keleeja glanced up at the house. All lay in darkness except for the outside motion-censored lights. "Are you sure he's home?"

"He's here."

She expected Daniel to knock on the door or ring the bell. He let himself in with a key. That started her wondering if they were roommates, but he explained.

"If I knock, he won't answer."

"What if he's just getting out of the shower?"

He chuckled. "I doubt he'll be wandering around the house naked, but if you're worried you can stay here until I check."

She laughed. "I'll close my eyes."

She stepped into the house after him and was struck with the scent of stale air and dirty clothes. Trying not to gag, she looked over at Daniel. He didn't seem to notice the odor. Men. Probably couldn't even smell it.

At least I can be reasonably sure he isn't just out of the shower.

She followed Daniel down a short dark hall. He clicked the light on in what turned out to be a living room, and there he was. Colin had been sitting in the darkness—fully clothed—pale, thin, and miserable.

CHAPTER 8

"Can you look in that cabinet right there and give me the salt?" Daniel pointed.

After a couple wrong choices, Keleeja found the right cabinet and handed over the salt. Daniel shook some on the steaks he prepared and then readied the frying pan.

"Shouldn't you let those sit a while. They'll be tough if you cook it too soon."

"I took them out just before coming to get you. Should be fine." He winked at her. "I've got a portfolio of several meals I can cook."

"Portfolio?" She looked at him like he was crazy.

"I'm not joking. I took pictures and printed them out. I keep them in a notebook just for my own satisfaction. Maybe I'll show you sometime."

"You're an odd one."

"Isabella didn't cook. In fact, she didn't do many things one might expect. She was more interested---uh never mind about her."

Disappointment stirred in her a bit. He wasn't ready for a new relationship. The fact that he kept bringing up his ex proved it.

She decided to change the subject, reminding herself that she was just here to spend the time in adult company and conversation. "What are we having with the steak?"

"I filled the fridge with groceries yesterday. There should be ingredients for salad if you'd like to help."

She opened the fridge. "If all you have is lettuce and tomatoes, I'm going to be very disappointed in you."

He laughed.

As soon as she saw the offerings, she knew right away what she would make. The corn and avocado salad she made a few weeks ago didn't go over well with the girls. A couple of them didn't like the taste of avocado. Lola stubbornly picked out all the bacon and left the lettuce. All four girls complained about the radishes, and only Keleeja scoffed down every bite.

Tonight, with just adults to feed, she figured the salad would be a hit. So she started on a pan of bacon while she prepped corn on the cob, scallions, radishes, avocado, and romaine.

"I'll leave out the anchovies this time too," she muttered to herself.

"I like anchovies."

"You would."

He looked over at her. "Would I?"

"You give me that impression."

"Of a man who likes anything?"

"Unconventional."

"Hm."

They worked side-by-side until the steaks rested on plates and Keleeja had finished tossing salad in a gigantic wooden bowl.

"Cobb salad?" he said, checking it out.

"Similar but not exactly. I hope you and Colin like it."

"I'm sure we will. Even if I don't prefer it, it's food."

"Encouraging." She rolled her eyes, and he grinned.

He had such a nice smile, straight teeth, white. Although she wondered what he really thought about everything. He came across as straightforward but kind. Was that the real him? What made him mad? Did he shout? What made him laugh?

"Come on. Let's get this in the dining room. You carry Colin's feet while I get him under the arms."

"What?"

The bark of laughter surprised her. "I was joking. I'll threaten him to get him to the table. After that, well, let's hope he takes a few bites."

So not romantic.

Keleeja sat at the table to the right of Colin with Daniel across from her. Colin frowned at the food and then at her. Annoyance rose in her, but she tamped it down. The man was grieving. She didn't need to take everything personally. Besides, she wasn't the one who cooked the meat.

"Daniel, I told you I didn't feel like seeing anyone and you bring a guest?"

"You're welcome. Keleeja and I met on one of my jobs. I told you... but you've got a lot on your mind."

Colin's eyebrows rose. *"A customer?"*

"No. The story is more stimulating than that. Maybe I'll tell you again—when you're really interested."

Colin grumbled under his breath. To her surprise, he served himself a little salad and a piece of steak. Keleeja didn't blame him. The scent of the beef teased her nose and made her stomach growl.

Keleeja realized what Daniel said and wondered just how interesting the night they met could be with her date dumping her like a bag of trash and Tawney being ill.

Colin's silver gaze trained on her. "Why would you accept his invitation to come to my house? You must feel awkward right now."

She pressed her lips together. "I wouldn't feel awkward if you weren't coming at me from the minute I walked through the door."

A spark of light twinkled in his eyes, but he doused it, frowning deeper. "One expects people to recognize when they're not wanted."

"Wow, are you always this friendly, or is it a special show just for me?"

"Guys, enough," Daniel interjected. "Stop bullying her, Colin. It's not her fault I brought her here."

"On a date."

"I've never been conventional."

"That's for sure." Colin tasted his food and ate a few bites. Keleeja noticed Daniel relax a little. She imagined he'd worried about his friend.

Conversation died down for a while as they each

enjoyed their dinner. Keleeja tried to fill in the void. "Daniel, this steak is delicious. It's so tender and juicy."

"There are a few things I do well," he bragged.

She laughed, shaking her head.

At her laugh, Colin looked up at her again. She sensed his resentment that she could laugh so easily. She wanted to tell him everyone had their challenges. It's what one did with the lemons and all that. But if she spoke her thoughts on the subject, he'd probably think she was being patronizing.

He's right about me feeling awkward. I want to stay. I want to go.

"I told you Colin works as a private investigator," Daniel said. "He owns his own firm."

"Both of you are self-employed." She sighed. "I wish I was brave enough to do that. I work for an insurance company. It pays well. I've been there since I left high school, but I'd love my own schedule."

"Colin," Daniel said, "do you want to ask her any questions?"

"What questions would I need to ask that I couldn't get the answers to in my own way?"

She clicked on what he meant. He let her know if she lied at any point, he would know because of his skills. For all she knew, he probably already did a background check on her and knew all her business.

What a jerk. Even as she told herself he shouldn't be blamed for how he acted in this difficult time, she couldn't stem the negative emotions toward him. Without the injury to his fiancée, he probably walked around with a superior attitude.

She studied Daniel as he ate with a big appetite. Every now and then he met her gaze and smiled. His eyes were full of openness and friendliness, and she liked him more. He was sweet and honest, exactly what attracted her to a guy. Not like his jerk of a friend.

When dinner was over, Keleeja offered to clear off the table and stack the dishes in the dishwasher. Daniel excused himself to use the restroom, and Colin sat like a lump at the table as if he forgot he wasn't alone.

She carried in all the plates and returned for the salad bowl. They had eaten only half. There would be plenty for tomorrow.

"Why are you here?" Colin said.

She stopped cold.

He eyed her. "You have four little sisters. Your mother is missing. There's no father to speak of."

She *knew* he'd done a background check! Her sisters' fathers never came up in her and Daniel's conversations. "You already know I'm here on a date with Daniel, and it wasn't my decision to come to your house. It was his. Take it up with your friend."

"I meant 'here' in the sense of seeing Daniel. Are you looking for a sugar daddy?"

She had flashbacks of the disastrous date who assumed she slept around and gave birth to four kids from four different dads. "Why don't you mind your business? I've been reminding myself that you're hurting more than I can imagine. But I don't deserve to be treated like trash because of it."

"I simply—"

"I don't want to hear it. You didn't throw us out.

You ate the food we cooked. I assume that means you love Daniel. So why don't you take the extra step and stop insulting the person he's seeing? For his sake if not mine."

He cracked a tiny smile. "You've got a lot of fire."

"That's right. I have to because I'm the barrier between my sisters and the world. And to answer your question, I'm not looking for anything or anyone. My situation isn't ideal for ninety-nine percent of the men out there. I'm here because I thought I'd enjoy some adult conversation for one night."

He full on smiled, and it threw her for a loop. He was cute too, in a less perfect way but still knee-weakening. "So thanks for nothing, then?"

She laughed. "It wasn't all bad. We had a few pockets there of decent conversation."

"Sorry."

His apology startled her, both for its suddenness and its sincerity. "What?"

He stood and shook himself then ran a hand over his head. The wince said he noticed how greasy his hair was. Who knew how long it had been since he washed it. "I apologize for treating you like 'trash.' I don't go around looking down on others—unless they deserve it."

The man read minds. Probably came handy with the kind of work he did.

"I'll forgive you this time." She started to leave the dining room when he stopped her.

"Fair warning though."

Here it came. He'd tell her if she hurt his friend, she would have him to deal with.

"Daniel is damaged in his own way. Isabella did a number on him. He's all smiles and friendliness, but deep inside is a man who's been burned. This is probably the worst time for him to get into another relationship since he hasn't gotten his head together yet."

"I'm not… We're not…" It did no good denying her attraction to Daniel and that she had expectations. Men and women in close contact were bound to develop feelings on one side or the other. "Thanks for the warning. I know how to control my own heart."

He shrugged. "Your funeral."

"So how did it go Friday?"

Keleeja and Autumn stood in her kitchen with the girls, preparing their usual Sunday dinner with all the fixings along with an elaborate dessert. This time, they'd chosen to cook beef stir fry with broccoli and noodles. Although mac and cheese didn't go with the beef stir fry traditionally, Keleeja never failed to make that dish on Sundays because Lara could live off it.

For dessert, Keleeja let the girls choose what they wanted to make, and the group all agreed on chocolate sponge cake. While Keleeja worked on the beef, Autumn helped the girls with the cake. Their shirts were already coated in flour, and chocolate lined each of their mouths.

"Okay, I guess." Keleeja eyed her sisters. "How much of that chocolate got into the bowl?"

"All of it," Lola lied proudly.

"Well, what's that around your mouth?"

She shrugged, maintaining her innocence. Keleeja laughed and went back to slicing the flank steak into thin strips. Next, she marinated the strips in a mixture of soy sauce and cornstarch. She would leave the meat in the marinade for no longer than an hour. No matter how many times she told herself to prepare the meat earlier, she forgot because something else took her attention.

"The 'you-know-what' went okay, but it could have been better," Keleeja explained. "His friend was rude one minute and considerate the next. Then after dinner, he disappeared because his fiancée called him. He never came back."

"Wow, and Daniel thought it was a good idea to take you over there? Wait, maybe his whole intention was to make the 'you-know-what' as bad as possible so you guys wouldn't work out."

"That's a thought."

"Lee, what's a 'you-know-what'?" Lola scooted her stool closer to Autumn and climbed on it to stick a finger in the cake batter.

Autumn gently tapped her hand. "Get out of there."

"It's a none of your business," Keleeja told her. "You're probably right, but he was the one who asked me to go. Why sabotage it?"

"I don't understand a man's mind. If I did, I'd have a promotion by now."

"So what were you guys up to at work?"

"Setting a trap."

"What *kind* of trap. Would you please elaborate and stop with the cryptic hints."

The girls distracted Autumn for a few minutes, clamoring over who got to lick the bowl and the mixer paddle. "I found out my boss has screwed over several other ladies in the company. We started talking in the break room and one of the ladies mentioned he has some bad habits no one knows about."

"Illegal habits?"

The doorbell rang. Keleeja frowned. She wasn't expecting anyone. Not on Sunday. That day was about family. Not that they received many visitors. But during the week and on Saturday, other kids in the neighborhood stopped by to play with the girls. Keleeja kept a strong rule that Sunday morning and afternoon was for family only.

"I'll get it," Lola shouted and jumped down from her stool. She started to run out of the kitchen.

"Freeze."

Lola froze. "I can unlock the door if I get on my stool."

"Thanks for letting me know, and if I catch you unlocking the door, you're in for it, miss."

Lola whined.

"Whew." Autumn dragged the back of a hand over her brow. "She's busy all day and all night."

"The ringleader," Keleeja agreed. She opened the front door to find none other than Daniel standing there with a bouquet of flowers in hand. "Daniel. What are you doing here?"

"Is this a bad time? I was in the neighborhood."

She flicked an eyebrow up at him. "Uh-huh."

"So it is a bad time?"

"Come in."

He stepped past her.

"It's not a bad time. We were cooking dinner."

He checked his cell phone. "It's eleven in the morning."

She laughed. "We've been calling it dinner on Sunday as far back as I can remember, and it's always as late as two in the afternoon or as early as noon. Whenever the food is ready, that's when we eat."

"Cool tradition. I like it."

Tawney appeared at her side and stuck her hand in Keleeja's. "Is he going to be family now, Lee?"

"What?" Keleeja's voice cracked.

Tawney ducked a bit more behind her but stared at Daniel around Keleeja's hip. "Sunday is for family."

"Oh." Daniel reddened. "I'm sorry. I should have called. I'll go."

"Stay." She didn't know what came over her. She certainly wasn't trying to give the kids ideas that he would be around. Sometimes it saddened her to think that there wasn't one man in their lives who was stable and a good influence. What would become of her sisters when they grew up without a male influence and example?

I'll just have to be everything to them and teach them what's acceptable and what isn't.

Easier said than done when she melted at sight of Daniel and threw all their traditions to the side for one of his smiles. So frustrating.

He joined them in the kitchen after she thanked him for the flowers.

"Oh, flowers. Pretty," Autumn commented. "I'll put them in water for you."

"It's Daniel," Lola called out. "Hi, Daniel."

"Hi, Daniel," Lara and Lily parroted.

Daniel's eyes glowed with pleasure that they remembered him. "Hey, girls. Good to see you again. I hear you're cooking dinner."

"We're making cake," Lara corrected him.

"You can make the chocolate cookies," Lola told him.

Keleeja shook her head. "We aren't making cookies this time."

Lola, back on her stool at the counter, crooked a finger at Daniel. He bent toward her, and she tucked a hand beside her mouth to whisper. "If you tell Lee you want cookies, she'll let you make them."

Keleeja suppressed a laugh. Lola had no idea she spoke loud enough for everyone in the kitchen to hear.

"Is that right?" Daniel said and looked at Keleeja.

"No cookies, Lola. You like chocolate cake. That's what we all voted on this week."

"We could have cake *and* cookies," she pleaded.

"I said no."

Lola grumbled.

Daniel moaned. "I have a feeling I lost points over the cookies."

Keleeja laughed. "Don't worry about it. She'll be on something else in a minute. So what do you cook other than steak?"

He shrugged. "A handful of my favorites, one of them being lasagna."

"You make lasagna?"

"I do. Girls, do you like lasagna?"

"Yes," they chorused.

"Anything with lots of cheese," Keleeja said. "Except Tawney, who has a little bit of a problem with dairy. Not severely, but we limit it with her."

He nodded and glanced down at the little one. Tawney crept away from Keleeja's side toward him. She found the courage to whisper, "Do you like chocolate?"

"Definitely. Can I have some of your cake when it's ready?"

"Yes."

Daniel turned his attention back to Keleeja. "I thought I remembered her having ice cream the other day."

"I got her a non-dairy one. They have three different flavors she can choose from. But sometimes, I let her have a very small special treat, and she takes digestive enzymes to help tolerate it."

Keleeja stopped speaking. What in the world was she doing sharing all the details of Tawney's health challenges. He wasn't interested in that. Worse, it must put him off thinking she didn't just have four little girls to raise. One of them suffered health issues. He must think Tawney was sickly since it wasn't all that long ago when Tawney had a fever and had to go to the hospital.

"Tawney isn't sickly," she blurted out. "She rarely gets a cold."

His eyes widened at her sudden outburst, and she kicked herself for trying too hard.

"I didn't think she was." He laid a gentle hand on top of Tawney's head. At some point, she had moved to stand right beside him. "She looks strong and healthy."

He's charmed shy little Tawney in seconds. Be careful, Keleeja.

They finished making dinner. When the cake came out of the oven, Autumn set in on a baking rack to cool.

"We'll frost it later," Keleeja said. "Girls, go wash your hands and clean your faces so we can eat. Daniel, are you staying to eat?"

"If that's okay?"

"Sure." She tried to sound offhand, but pleasure and warmth spread through her system.

Autumn went to supervise the girls in their cleanup, leaving Keleeja and Daniel alone in the kitchen.

"I like your home." He scanned the chaos that the girls left in the kitchen. Flour all over the counter and floor, eggshells cracking underfoot, stools everywhere to trip over, and the sink piled up with dishes. "It's warm and lived-in."

"You mean it's a mess. I gave up trying to clean while we're cooking because the girls make messes as fast as I can clean them. Maybe when they're a little older, we'll do better."

"I didn't mean messy. I meant, it looks like the kind of place you want to raise your family in. You've made it exactly what it should be, and that's what I like."

"Thanks." She placed all the stools back where they

belonged in the pantry and grabbed the broom from the closet. "I had this friend from school who I used to visit sometimes. Her parents kept their house immaculate. It looked like a museum in there, and I used to dream that one day I would have a house like that. It never happened, and now I don't care. This works."

He looked thoughtful.

"What?"

"My house doesn't look like a museum, more like something out of a home interiors magazine. I had nothing to do with it."

His ex-wife again. She hesitated and then spoke what was on her mind. "You bring up your ex-wife a lot. I wonder if you're ready to date when you're still in love with her. Maybe you should try to work things out."

Anger sparked in the green eyes, and his jaw flexed. "Perhaps you shouldn't speak on subjects you know nothing about."

She gasped. Wow, zero to sixty in seconds. Daniel Morgan could get angry. Good to know.

CHAPTER 10

"I'm sorry. I can't believe I said that."

The anger in his eyes and tension in his stance disappeared without a trace. She wondered if she imagined it. Before she could respond, the kids and Autumn returned from the bathroom. A flurry of activity ensued with them setting the table and the girls running around changing their minds about where they wanted to sit.

"You can sit over here, Daniel." Lola struggled with one of the chairs, scraping it over the floor.

Daniel rushed to help her and then gestured. "Why don't you take it, and I'll sit next to you. How's that?"

Lola flushed. She ignored his gesture and moved to the seat she always took up, which was at Keleeja's right side. All the others fell into their normal spots. What was even the point of them playing musical chairs?

Daniel ended up next to Tawney, who sat on Keleeja's left, while Autumn took up the opposite end of the table. The triplets lined the right side of the table. Sometimes, Keleeja imagined the usual two empty seats being taken up with her husband and a little one of her own. She tried not to see Daniel as having potential as her husband. Not after that slight argument, that's for sure.

"Who's saying the blessing?" Keleeja asked.

"I will!" Lily threw her hand high in the air, waving it like Keleeja couldn't see her.

"Okay, Lily. Go ahead."

Daniel's gaze filled with amusement and interest as he watched Lily fold her hands and shut her eyes. All the rest of the heads bowed, but Keleeja peeked at Daniel.

"Lord, bless the food and bless the cooks—*us*. And…" She meandered around a bit. Keleeja started to make a suggestion when Lily continued in earnest. "And get Daniel to like our food because it's good. Amen."

Keleeja, Daniel, and Autumn laughed.

"I'm sure I'll enjoy the food, Lily," Daniel said.

"The funny never ends here," Autumn told him.

"I see."

They dug in, and Keleeja's mind wandered again. She let Autumn and Daniel carry the conversation. Daniel tried to include the girls in simple discussions. Even shy little Tawney joined in. Keleeja sighed in contentment.

Crash!

Keleeja startled to attention. Tears filled Lara's eyes, and she stared wide-eyed at Keleeja.

"What were you doing with a glass, Lara?"

"I was thirsty."

Keleeja got up to grab a towel and began sopping up the spilled liquid around Lara's plate. Some of it had gone into the plate and made a brown moat around Lara's mac and cheese.

"I know you were thirsty, baby. I'm saying why were you using a glass instead of plastic? I thought I set a plastic glass in your spot." Keleeja kicked herself for not paying attention. Come to think of it, she wasn't the one to pour Lara's sweet tea.

"That's my fault," Daniel apologized. "She said she was thirsty, and I grabbed the nearest empty glass and gave her some tea."

"It's okay. You didn't know. We don't give Lara glass. Actually we don't give *any* of them glass to drink from." She mouthed to him *'especially Lara'* over the little girl's head. If it was up to Lara, Keleeja would soon have no breakable dishes in the house. Her fingers let any and everything slip through them. Keleeja hoped she would eventually grow out of her clumsiness.

After dinner, the girls played in their rooms, and Autumn collapsed in the sunroom to watch TV. Keleeja looked in on her. "Hey, do you mind if we go for a quick walk?"

Autumn waved her off. "Go right ahead. They'll be getting ready for a nap soon, and I'm getting into this movie."

"Thanks, Autumn. I appreciate it."

Out on the street, Keleeja strolled next to Daniel

and tried to think how she could bring up the subject of his ex-wife without making him mad.

"About earlier," he began, reading her mind. "I'm sorry again."

"Don't. It's fine."

"It's not fine." He ran fingers through his hair.

She wondered what it would be like to do that herself, to touch him, and then wrestled her thoughts under control.

"You're probably right. I might not be ready to date."

Disappointment kept her mute.

"I hate to admit it. I'm not in love with Isabella, but our breakup affected me."

"Colin mentioned something."

"Like what?"

"That you're broken."

He frowned.

"Are you thinking he's one to talk?"

He grinned. "Something like that."

"Do you wish you two were still together?"

"Not really. She wasn't what I thought she was, and that makes me angry."

She nodded.

He stopped walking and faced her. Her heartrate kicked up, although she had no idea what he was about to say.

"I haven't known you long, but I can tell you're not like her. At the same time, I question if I know any better. I was deceived for years, thinking she and I had the same dreams."

Keleeja waited for him to continue. The more he talked, the more she could learn about what he wanted from a relationship with her. Or if one was possible down the line. He didn't run off after learning about the girls. Maybe this was why. He felt safe to see Keleeja because there was no danger in falling for her.

The new thought struck her dumb, and she almost missed Daniel's next admission.

"Isabella cheated. The entire time I thought we were trying for kids and failing, she was making sure it didn't happen."

"Oh wow, that's horrible. I'm sorry."

"I wanted children desperately."

"'Desperately'?" She didn't know what to think about that.

"I grew up in the foster care system. All I ever wanted was to have a family of my own someday."

Keleeja's heart cracked. "And she tricked someone like you with a dream like that. How could she live with herself? At the very least if she didn't want kids, she should have loved you enough to not marry you."

He blinked at her.

"Sorry. Don't be mad. I shouldn't have said that about your marriage. I don't know all the details, and no one needs my two cents."

"No, you're right. Plus, I brought the conversation up. Why shouldn't you give your opinion?"

They started walking again.

"Fact is, loving someone doesn't make you selfless."

"You believe she loved you?"

"Yes, in the beginning. But Isabella is a very narcissistic person. She always put herself first. I didn't notice until much later."

"Because you set your sights on that family." She hesitated. "You're not doing the same thing all over?"

"What do you mean?"

"You're not thinking of my sisters being that family you never had?"

He frowned. "You say whatever pops into your head, don't you? No holding back."

She groaned. "It's a hazard of raising the girls. *They* always speak their mind, and it's rubbed off on me. You know what, we had a good time at lunch, but maybe it's time to say goodbye."

"You're right."

"Our first date was weird. Now this. So…"

"Message received. Thanks for lunch, Keleeja." He strolled off toward her house and his car, parked in her driveway. She took her time walking back to the house, went up to her room, and dropped onto the bed to try to sleep away the rest of a lousy day.

CHAPTER 11

"Why in in the world am I here with you, Autumn?" Keleeja strained to hear if someone else was nearby. The entire floor where Autumn worked seemed to be abandoned. A few of the lights weren't turned on yet, so shadows stretched everywhere. Paranoia made Keleeja's skin tingle. She felt like any second someone would spring out and demand to know what they were doing.

"Because everyone backed out of our plan, and I need a lookout." Autumn carried a huge bag on her shoulder as she marched ahead of Keleeja down an aisle lined on both sides with cubicles. Her friend usually carried a big bag, but this one was ridiculous.

"Maybe you should have taken the hint and decided against this hairbrained scheme. I'm not going to jail for you."

"We won't go to jail. And you have plausible deni-ability."

"How you figure? I'm here at a company I don't work at—before usual business hours. They probably have security cameras outside that already recorded me coming in. And what's in that bag? It's big even by your standards."

Autumn paused to dig through the bag. Today she was the height of professionalism in a gray pinstriped pantsuit with medium heels. She had swept her long hair up on top of her head and pinned it into place. Any other day, she would have dressed business casual, but today was special.

"I thought about wearing all black with sneakers and a ball cap, but if someone comes in early, I'd have to explain the getup."

"All black? Girl, you need to cut back on the movies. And why would you need to dress like a cat burglar? Please tell me you didn't drag me up here to break into the company safe."

"I'm not aware we have a safe. *Now* who sounds like a movie addict?" She patted the side of her bag and grinned. "I have just the thing in here. Come on."

"Nope."

Autumn started to walk on but stopped at Keleeja's refusal. "What?"

"I'm not going another step until you explain in detail what you're planning to do."

"Lee, we don't have much time. The early birds will be arriving soon."

Keleeja tapped her foot.

Her friend sighed. "You've been in a mood since

yesterday afternoon. What happened with Daniel? Why wouldn't you talk to me about it?"

"There's nothing to talk about. Just me, destined for spinsterhood."

"You don't know that."

"Stop changing the subject, Autumn. Tell me what you're going to do, or I'm leaving. I've got to be at work in an hour."

"I thought we said we would have each other's back no matter what?"

Keleeja grumbled under her breath, unmoving.

"Fine. I'm going to bug his office."

"What?"

"Shh! Keep your voice down."

They both listened to the area around them. A machine whirred in the distance, but that might be automatic.

Autumn tugged at her blouse, wrinkling the material. "It's all I can think of. Logic won't work with this man."

"Have you tried?"

"Lee."

"I'm just asking."

"I'm going to do it no matter what. Even if I'm the only one, I'll follow through."

"Your stubborn trait is why they should have promoted you."

"That's right." Autumn waggled her head in the affirmative, her thin pink lips pressed tight. "I'm going to catch him, Lee. I promise you that."

"Okay, then what? You're going to the police? Blackmail him for your promotion?"

Autumn paled. "I haven't thought that far ahead."

"Sweetheart, don't we have enough drama in our lives without this?"

"Will you help me or not?"

"Fine. I'll be lookout, but if we're caught, and I go to jail and my babies get put in foster care—I will skin you!"

A short while later, Keleeja stood outside Autumn's boss's office, feeling way too obvious. What would she even say if someone questioned her? What excuse could she give, especially not being one of their employees?

As she pondered the subject, an elevator dinged. Her stomach dropped into her toes, and her mouth dried. She flung the office door open and squeaked, "Autumn, someone's coming!"

"I need more time." Autumn stood on the back of one of the upholstered chairs with bare feet. She stretched to tiptoe so she could reach the top of a cabinet. Something black and silver slipped from view, and Keleeja assumed it was a camera. "I haven't even tested the angle yet."

"Do you want to test it in jail?"

Autumn grumbled. "Buy me more time."

"Are you crazy?"

"Please, Lee."

Keleeja shut the office door and drew in a deep breath. It was a good thing the office had frosted windows.

Anyone looking in would see shadows and nothing else. If Autumn kept still, no one could tell she was there. Keleeja needed to make sure the coast was clear until Autumn was done, and this ridiculous escapade could end. Why did she give in that crazy woman?

She made her way down an aisle, nervous that whoever got off the elevator was at that moment traveling a different direction.

Calm down, Keleeja. It's not like you couldn't see their head over the cubicle walls.

"They might be super short," she muttered.

"Good morning."

She jumped a mile.

"Oh sorry. I didn't mean to startle you." The last person she wanted to see stood before her—Autumn's boss. Talk about bad luck. The man whose hairline began behind his ears was thin except for a round belly. He might be an inch shorter than Keleeja, but he stood tall and straight like he wanted to intimidate anyone in his path.

Keleeja had met him two years ago at a company picnic Autumn dragged her to. He struck her as a man who had zero idea he wasn't good looking. Then again, she admired anyone who felt confident in themselves no matter their appearance.

He waggled a finger at her. "You're Keleeja, right? Autumn's friend?"

She gaped. He remembered her name after two years? And it wasn't like her name was a common one. She was impressed. "Um…"

He grinned. "I never forget a beautiful face—or figure."

She cringed inwardly. "Oh, hey, Mr. Um…"

His grin faltered at bit, and his eyebrows rose. This guy was genuinely surprised she didn't remember him in return. She did, but he didn't need to know that.

"You don't remember me. I'm Autumn's supervisor, Jeff Slathers."

"Oh, hello, Mr. Slathers."

He stepped closer and extended a hand, expecting her to take it. She did, with reluctance, and he held on, patting hers with his other hand.

"Call me Jeff. What brings you to the office so early? Where's Autumn?" He stretched a bit to look over her shoulder. Her stomach dropped, and her tongue tied. She couldn't think of the lie she'd come up with.

"She um… She uh…" Jeez, she was terrible at subterfuge. That was a good thing, but really in a pinch, one would think her brain would work—self-preservation and all that. "I have to get going. I'm due at work in an hour."

She tugged her hand in his, but his grip tightened. He moved even closer, watching her face like he read her mind. "Don't go. Why don't we have a little chat?"

Her head spun. He was on to them. One of the people who dropped out of the plot must have talked. She could just see the jail cell closing in on her and her little sisters crying as the State took them away.

She opened her mouth to confess.

"I've always found Black women to be very attractive," Jess said. "And you, you're especially beautiful. I bet you have your choice of men every week."

The confession died on her tongue. All of a sudden, she knew what Jeff's bad habits were, which Autumn tried to catch on film. He used his position to corner women and make them submit to his disgusting desires.

She licked her lips and stood straighter, jerking her hand from his. Did he imagine he had cornered *her* because she couldn't come up with an excuse of why she was there? Did he think she would go along with whatever he suggested, like going to his office and— her stomach turned, threatening to reject the breakfast she'd eaten earlier.

"I appreciate the compliments, sir, but they're inappropriate. Please keep your comments about my appearance to yourself."

"Aw, don't be like that, Keleeja." He had the nerve to pout. *Gross.* A man poking his bottom like out like she was supposed to fall for it. Didn't anyone ever tell him that cute little move was for women alone? Talk about a weirdo.

"Excuse me, Mr. Slathers. I have to get moving. Just let me tell Autumn I'm going." She raised her voice on that last bit, hoping she wasn't being too obvious. As soon as she was out of sight from this fool, she'd phone her friend and pray Autumn heard her warning. There was no telling if the boss' office was soundproof.

"Lee! I *did* bring your book to the office. Sorry about that. Here it is." Autumn appeared, waving a book in the air that Keleeja had never seen before, let alone had any interest in reading. "Good morning, Jeff. You're in bright and early."

Jeff's face reddened. "I have a meeting. Good morning, Autumn. Excuse me. I'd better get my notes."

He rushed past Autumn and disappeared around a corner. A door opened and closed, and Keleeja breathed a sigh of relief. Her legs almost gave out, but Autumn grabbed her arm and grinned.

"We did it, Lee. I can't believe we did it. We pulled off a job you only see in movies."

"Yeah, and I'm leaving it there from now on." Keleeja moaned, wiping a hand over her moist brow. "I thought I was going to throw up dealing with your boss."

Autumn frowned. "He didn't do anything inappropriate, did he?"

"He kept talking about how beautiful I am and wanting to have a chat."

"Don't go anywhere with him."

"Like I was? What would he do if I did?"

"You don't want to know." Autumn hooked her arm through Keleeja's and turned her around. "Come on. I'll walk you downstairs."

"Did you get your camera into position at least?"

"Yup. Let me show you."

Autumn rode with her in the elevator while pointing out on her phone how her camera picked up everything that Jeff did and said in his office. The view included most of the space, especially the couch, and Keleeja shuddered to think what kind of use that thing got. She hoped her imagination got the better of her and things didn't go that far.

"I can stop and start the recording from my phone. Isn't that wild? I never knew this kind of thing was possible and that I could afford it." Autumn laughed. "The internet is amazing."

Keleeja agreed, but she wondered if Autumn tried to catch Jeff because of losing her promotion or if there was a deeper reason. She decided to press her friend later for the full story and help her any way she could.

CHAPTER 12

"Ooooh, Lily. I'm telling. You can't bite that."

Keleeja knocked on a cantaloupe to check for ripeness when she heard Lola's voice. She spun around.

"What are you doing, Lily?" Keleeja spotted the apple Lily tried to hide behind her back. "You know better, Lily. We haven't paid for that fruit. Put it back, and don't you dare bite it."

"She already did," Tattle-tale Lola declared. She was in state this morning, getting on Keleeja's nerves.

Keleeja marched over to her little sister and grabbed the apple. Lily's eyes widened in alarm. Sure enough she found a small bite in the shape of Lily's mouth. She sighed. "I thought this would be a special treat, getting out here to the farmer's market early on a Saturday morning. All I've dealt with is whining, tattling, and thievery." She pointed out each offender as she spoke.

The only one not driving her bananas for a change was Tawney. Keleeja thanked God the oldest of the little ones was on her best behavior today. Then she remembered that Tawney's sixth birthday was coming up. Keleeja warned her to behave and she would get something special.

If only the triplets' birthday was near. Too much to ask for, I guess.

"That's it. We're getting out of here. I've had enough for one morning. Grab hands."

After Keleeja paid for the apple, they weaved through the aisles of fruit and honey stalls to get to the outside of the pavilion and further toward the parking lot. As they went, Keleeja caught an older woman's eye, one of the vendors. The woman smiled fondly at Keleeja and the girls.

"I just love seeing young mothers and their little ones making healthy choices. And they're so cute too," the woman gushed. "Here. Make something special for them with these strawberries."

"Thanks but—"

"On the house. Just for warming an old woman's heart."

"Yay, strawberries!" Lola shouted, and her sisters showed equal enthusiasm.

"Say thank you, girls." Keleeja accepted the small basket of strawberries and tucked it into the bag she'd brought along for her purchases.

Soon they were back on the road, headed toward the other side of town. She wished the biggest local farmer's market was closer to home. They had a thirty-minute drive each way, which was why the visit was a special treat.

"What are you going to make with the strawberries, Lee?" Lola had no shame about her earlier attitude. "Pancakes?"

"That's what you want," Keleeja said.

"Yes."

Keleeja laughed. "That was rhetorical."

"What's reto…?"

"Never mind."

"How about strawberry short cake?" Tawney suggested.

"I just made a strawberry box cake last week."

"It's all gone," Lola complained.

Keleeja rolled her eyes. She thought about the day her mom introduced the girls to candy. After an all-night date with one of her boyfriends, she came home with an apology gift. The gift turned out to be a bag full of candy. Before then, the girls didn't know much about junk food, especially candy. After that, they were hooked on sugar, and Keleeja blamed her mom every time she recalled it.

"What about oatmeal for breakfast tomorrow with strawberries in it?"

Everyone groaned except Lara, the one with the simplest palette.

"I'll think of something, but this is as good a time as any to stop off at the grocery store to grab a few things."

Normally, she would have waited until she was

closer to home, but she was just driving past a grocery store and figured she'd stop in. They parked and climbed out of the car.

"No running, screaming, or tattling—unless it's an emergency. Oh and no eating stuff I haven't paid for. Do you hear me, girls?"

"Yes," they sang.

A horn blasted as they were passing a car, and she squeaked in alarm. When the horn kept sounding off, she looked around, checking that each of the girls were close to her side and safe. Then she bent to peer into the car where the jerk kept pounding the horn. The big hands, the dark messy hair, and especially the frowning mouth all looked familiar. It took her a minute to realize where she knew him from.

"Get back in the car, girls."

"But I want cereal!"

Keleeja hardly paid attention to who made the demand. She herded her sisters into her car and locked the doors. "One minute," she called to them and ran around to the driver side of the guy's car.

She knocked on the window. He slammed a fist on the steering wheel. Even though she saw him do it, she jumped again. She seriously had to calm down. And he needed to stop.

"Colin!"

He looked around at her. The vacant silver gaze hardly registered her presence let alone recognition of who she was. She gestured for him to lower the window, but he didn't move.

She tried the door handle and found it unlocked.

"Colin, are you okay? It's me, Keleeja. I met you when—"

"She's gone."

The question died on her tongue unspoken. She knew who he meant. His fiancée died. The last Keleeja heard, he stayed with his fiancée after the accident, visiting her, talking to her on the phone. Daniel had told Keleeja the woman was in serious condition, but since she was in a rehabilitation facility, Keleeja assumed she would get better. Apparently, she was wrong.

With bags beneath his eyes and sallow skin, Colin looked like he hadn't slept in weeks. His clothes were rumbled, and his car was full of fast-food wrappers. At least he'd been eating.

His chin dipped, and he shut his eyes. When he began shaking, her heart went out to him. He made no sound, and she couldn't see his face behind the sheet of hair that needed a barber.

Instinct drove her to wrap her arms around him. "Everything's going to be okay, Colin. It'll take time, but it will get better."

He made an indistinct sound.

"You need someone by your side for a while. Where's Daniel?"

He didn't answer.

"Colin? Where's your best friend? You need him right now to help get you through this hardest part."

"He's got his own problems."

"Nothing more important than you. Did you call him and tell him?"

"No."

"*Colin.*"

"Doesn't matter."

"It *does* matter! Call him." She searched his car for his phone. When she didn't find it, she took out hers. Even though she hadn't spoken with Daniel in months—not since that last time they disagreed—she still had his number in her phone. "I'll call him, and you can talk to him."

"Don't bother." He looked up, anger simmering in his eyes. "He went back to her, that stupid Isabella."

Keleeja gasped.

"After all she did to him. After what I told him about her, he went back when her lover left her, and she came running to Daniel. I'm not calling him!"

"Fine. Then you're coming with us."

"What?" He blinked in disbelief at her.

She stood up straight. "Get what you need out of here. First, you're coming into the grocery store with us. Then, you're coming home with us. You're not in any condition to drive. And if there's someone you want me to call later, I'll do that. For now, move it."

She half expected him to buck against her command. Instead, his movements were sluggish as he obeyed. Like a zombie, he followed her and the girls into the grocery store. Tawney and Lara kept looking back at him, a question in their eyes.

Lola spoke right up. "Stranger danger, Lee."

Keleeja snorted. "Don't be silly, Lola. You know good and well I brought him in here. This is Colin, girls. Do you remember my friend Daniel?"

They chorused that they remembered.

"Well this is his friend. He's not feeling well, and we're going to look after him for a while."

"Does he have to go to the hospital?" Tawney wanted to know.

"No, sweetie. Now, shush, everyone. Let's concentrate on getting what we need and getting home."

Keleeja moved as fast as she could through the grocery store and had the entire group back in the car headed home. Although she kept an eye on Colin, he gave her no trouble. That didn't mean the grief-filled expression on his face didn't worry her.

At home, she herded the girls into the kitchen to help put away groceries. Over her shoulder, she called to Colin, "You can sit in the living room if you want. I'll be back in a second.

"He's not listening," Lola tattled.

Keleeja turned to find Colin had followed them again. He stood in her kitchen doorway taking in everything, from the sink piled with dishes to the open pantry door, displaying the disorder in there to the rings of grape juice stains on the table.

That morning, she'd been so eager to get to the farmer's market early, she hadn't done much clean up after breakfast.

Yeah, because normally you're so organized. Right.

Colin took a seat at the table, his hands hanging down between his legs. She wondered if he was hungry but didn't say. Lola invaded his personal space, staring into his eyes.

"Lola!"

"He wants pancakes, Lee."

"You read his mind, huh?"

"Lee, his mind isn't a book. How can I read it?"

Keleeja shook her head. "Like you can even read yet. Get out of his face, Lola. And we're not having pancakes. You girls ate a good breakfast not two hours ago. You're not hungry."

"What about the strawberries?"

"They'll keep."

Lola moaned.

After Keleeja got the girls out of the kitchen, she turned to Colin. "Are you hungry, Colin? I can make you something to eat. Whatever you want."

"No."

"No what?"

He didn't answer.

"When is the last time you ate, and I'm not talking about Mickey D's?"

Again nothing.

She sighed and decided to make him sausage and eggs with toast. Maybe he would eat it without thinking in the same way he followed her around the store. A few minutes later, just as she hoped, he picked his fork up and tucked in when she set the plate in front of him.

The food disappeared, but she couldn't tell if he liked it. Well, never mind. It was a start. She got him into the living room, and she turned on the music channel on the TV, an easy listening selection. A scented plugin chased away the smell of grease hanging in the air. She brought in a basket of laundry and began folding.

"Would you like to talk about her, Colin?"

"No."

That was different. She remembered the disagreement with Daniel was about his ex always being on his mind.

"I'm a good listener. It might help to—"

"No *feelings*." He bit the words out with a frown like the thought disgusted him.

"Fine!" Dang, he was disagreeable. She reminded herself he just lost the love of his life and wouldn't be at his best. Although she wondered if he had a best. Colin seemed like the kind of man who didn't care what others thought or how they felt. It was an unfair assumption, but she couldn't help thinking it.

His gaze wandered over to the clothes she folded. She smoothed one of the triplets' shorts after folding it then set it on a pile of others and moved on to a pink t-shirt with a unicorn on the front.

"They're all girls," he commented.

"Yup. A house full of girls. Does it intimidate you?" She grinned.

He blinked at her.

"No, nothing intimidates Colin… What's your last name?"

"Voss."

"Nothing intimidates Colin Voss."

He frowned. No, he frowned harder. She sighed and gave up. Let him do what he wanted. She'd just keep an eye on him enough to know he would be okay.

Throughout the rest of the day, she handled chores. Colin sometimes sat in the living room. Other times he followed her from room to room, standing in the doorway watching as she vacuumed or put toys away. His keen gaze took in everything, but she couldn't read his expression to know what he thought.

"Girls!" she shouted at one point. "Ugh, I've asked you not to leave these Legos everywhere. Do you realize how much they hurt to step on?"

"Yes," Lola said without looking up from doll she dressed and undressed. Keleeja shook her head.

"She's the one with the most personality." Colin stated the observation like he'd been studying the girls all day, which he had.

Keleeja didn't worry much about whether she invited some weirdo into her house with ulterior motives. She could spot that kind a mile off. Not to mention the fact that she never left the girls alone with him.

"I can't tell them apart," he went on.

She blinked in surprise. "What do you mean?"

He gestured toward Lola. "Is she Lara, Lily, Lola, or Tawney? I've heard you shout each of those names a hundred times."

"We're looking after you. Don't complain." She stripped the beds to prepare for changing them to fresh sheets. "And the triplets aren't identical, not to mention Tawney, who's two years older."

He rubbed his chin, thinking. It was the most

animation she'd seen out of him all day without prompting. "They *look* identical."

Her mouth fell open. He couldn't be serious. And wasn't he bragging the last time she met him that he was a good investigator or some such, that he never missed the details? The triplets looked alike in that they were easily family, but identical? No.

It was because he didn't care, she decided. Unlike Daniel, who was sensitive to others' feelings and kind, Colin couldn't be bothered with what didn't affect him personally. That was her bias against him, but she felt confident in the conclusion.

"The one with the personality as you put it is Lola. Always Lola. I pray daily for strength to deal with her and her mouth."

He nodded understanding, and she pointed out each of the others and named them. He paid attention and seemed to store the information away in his memory. His color improved a bit, and he stood a little stronger. Good.

He rubbed his belly. "Are you going to make them lunch?"

"You're already hungry again?"

"It's been hours."

"Well, it's good that you have an appetite." She balled the sheets up and threw them down the stairs outside the room. "I'll make lunch."

"Yay!" the girls shouted.

Keleeja should have known they were listening to everything she and Colin said.

"Can we have pancakes now, Lee?" Lola asked.

Keleeja gave up. "Yes, fine. Everyone agreed? Strawberry pancakes for lunch?"

The cheers rose, and she looked to Colin. He shrugged. "If it's edible, I'll eat it."

"I guess this is a two breakfast Saturday. I shouldn't be surprised."

CHAPTER 13

Colin toyed with his phone. He battled between calling Daniel to tell him about Sherrie and continuing like he was, just for today. He didn't know why he'd gone along with Keleeja's plan to take him to her place, especially with four little girls shouting over each other all day. He figured they had two volumes— off and high-pitched blast.

Not that he didn't like kids. He'd dreamed of having a couple with his fiancée sometime in the future. The idea seemed inevitable but not mandatory or time sensitive. He wasn't like Daniel, who lived and breathed the idea of family.

None of that mattered at the moment. It was all he could do to breathe, let alone dream. The noisy girls and bossy Keleeja distracted him from his grief. He could focus on them, and the pain might not kill him.

"More laundry?" He wrinkled his nose when Keleeja strolled into the living room a couple hours after lunch with another basket. "Does it end?"

"Have you seen how messy they are? No, it doesn't end. But what I like about doing laundry is you can do so many other things *while* you do it. So it's not really a hassle."

He wondered if Sherrie had liked doing laundry and couldn't remember. Come to think of it, whenever he visited, her apartment was always spotless. *She* was always spotless like she'd never had a hair out of place or a stain on a blouse in her life.

Keleeja stood barefoot in a pair of shorts and a faded tee with the hemline unraveling. The spot of white in her hair was likely flour from the pancakes. She didn't seem to mind that she didn't look her best. Maybe that was what Daniel liked in her.

No, that can't be it. He saw her first when she went out on a date with another man. I doubt she looked like this.

He studied her again.

"What are you staring at?" she demanded. "You want to help me fold?"

He raised his eyebrows. "Why would I?"

A shirt came flying at his head. "Here. Start with this one."

He considered throwing it back, but she might kick him out. If he went home, there was no telling what would happen. When she came along in that parking lot, he'd been close to losing it. Her commanding tone tore through the scald in his head and activated his movements. Now, after several hours in her and her sisters' company, he could do a little thinking. Better to stay. He started on the shirt.

"Seriously? Have you ever folded anything?" She rested a hand on her hip, watching him.

His face warmed. "I don't need to fold my shirts. I hang them in the closet."

"T-shirts too?"

"Yes."

She heaved a heavy sigh, something she had done several times regarding him. "Like this. Watch me."

Swallowing irritation, he mimicked her movements and came out with a decent fold—in his mind. She ripped the shirt away and did it herself. He grabbed it back, destroying her work and refolded better.

She laughed at him. "You're stubborn. Do you know that?"

"I've been told that once or twice."

"I bet it's every day. Do you have any siblings?"

The personal question took him by surprise, but he didn't mind sharing about family. "Two brothers, one sister."

"Do they know…about…"

"No."

"Colin!"

"They would smother me and push me to talk. I don't want to deal with that—*yet*."

"Alright. Are you the baby?"

He glared at her, and she laughed again. It wasn't a bad laugh, kind of pleasant. Her big brown eyes lit up, and that one slightly crooked tooth made the smile what it was. If she didn't have so many kids, she might have been married or at least involved by now. He knew men, and most if not all would run the other way when her brood came along.

"I'm the second one."

She nodded, no doubt analyzing him about being one of the middle kids and the psychology that went with that. Then again, maybe she took what he said as simple information and moved on.

Now I'm analyzing. What she thinks about me doesn't matter.

He took a pair pants from the pile and folded, careful not to leave wrinkles. Her face lit up, and he felt a ridiculous sense of accomplishment.

"Great job. Now you're getting the hang of it. I'll have you domesticated yet."

He cringed, and she burst out laughing.

"So kidding. Thanks for your help. Don't feel you have to do it though. You can do whatever you like."

"Is this what you do every weekend? Work?"

"No, not entirely. I get the weekly chores done, and then the girls and I have fun. Sunday is more of a free day. On Saturday, there's always something to do before we let loose."

"I'm sorry." He said the words quickly before he changed his mind. Watching her, talking to her, had pushed the grief back long enough to think of someone other than himself for a few moments.

"About what? Not folding laundry? Please, it's nothing. If you're talking about my life then—"

"I mean about asking you if you were looking for a sugar daddy."

Her eyebrows rose and drew his attention to a tiny

flaw on her forehead, a scar. "Oh right the night of the first date."

"I was being mean. Contrary to what you might think, it's not my nature. I can be tough when I need to be for work, but I'm not normally a jerk."

"Good to know. And your apology is accepted. You knew all about me without asking that night, didn't you? Your line of work makes you curious."

"You want to say 'nosy.'"

She snorted. "Okay, nosy. Intrusive, meddling…"

"Would you like to borrow my thesaurus?"

"You carry one around?"

He grunted.

"Oh! Do I detect a smile?"

"No."

The four girls ran into the room and stopped before him. Lola—he knew her face now—handed him a stack of playing cards and climbed up on the couch beside him. The other three dropped to the carpet around the coffee table with expectant expressions on their faces.

He looked at Keleeja.

"You can tell them you don't want to play, but how about five minutes?"

"Uno?"

"Haven't you played before?"

"Of course, but I meant do they know how to count?"

She laughed. "Fair question. Yes. The triplets can count pretty high, although they can't read yet. Tawney is learning and doing great. You don't have to know how to count to play. You recognize the color and number matches."

She had a good point. He didn't want to play cards. The weight in his chest held him down. At the same time, the way the girls responded to him—not intimidated—made him want to do it anyway. He wondered if they responded in the same way to Daniel. It was probably a personality thing, similar to their big sister.

"Right." He glanced down at Lola, sitting close to him. While her sisters patiently waited, Lola's expression said, 'get on with it already.' He had no idea why his brain saw them as identical when he first arrived. Each of the triplets had their own distinctive features. While it was obvious that they were related, they didn't look exactly alike. Even their heights were different.

He put his ignorance down to not spending enough time in the presence of his nieces and nephews, getting to know kids better. He sent them gifts and phoned on birthdays and visited with family at holidays but nothing more. His life had been taken up with his business and his fiancée.

Pain wrenched his gut, and he forced his thoughts outward to the girls waiting for him to play Uno. A quick dealing of the cards, and they began.

"Don't cheat," Lola warned him. "Because Lara cheats. She's sneaky."

"I am not!" Lara's coffee with cream complexion reddened. Her hazel eyes narrowed with anger. "You're the cheater, Lola. Lee says so."

"Okay, girls," Keleeja said. "If you're going to fight, you're not going to play."

Lola grumbled under her breath, and the anger Lara displayed dissipated within seconds. She bounced up and down, grinning as she viewed her cards. Lola leaned closer to Colin to see into his hand. No shame at all. It looked like Lara spoke the truth about her cheating.

Colin didn't normally go for cards, but he found it distracting, almost enjoyable, to watch the girls' faces when they were doing well or losing. They bounced up and down and punctuated every discard with a cheer as if it was a major accomplishment.

While they knew how to play the game, they weren't as shrewd about their moves as Colin. He saw several opportunities to trounce each of them. Keleeja read his mind and stared hard. When he felt her gaze on him, he looked up from his hand. She mouthed the words, *let them win.*

He frowned. She raised her eyebrows. He sensed the same warning she gave them. If he didn't play nice, he wouldn't play at all. His grumbled complaint didn't impress her. He gave in and lost one game after another. What started out as mildly entertaining turned into a real feat to lose to each of the girls so they could all lord it over him.

After what felt like an eternity, the girls grew bored and ran off to do something else. He slumped back against the couch and shut his eyes., breathing deeply.

"Exhausting, aren't they?" Keleeja teased.

He cracked an eye open at her. "I don't understand how you deal with this every day."

"Easy. I love them to pieces."

"Hmm."

The day turned to evening, and he stood at the window, looking out on the street. He should stop being a coward and go home. A taxi would take him back to his car. He imagined his house, which he'd purchased a couple years ago. Sherrie helped him choose it. She'd offered her opinions about what she did and didn't like, and although he didn't tell her at the time, her likes and dislikes were the deciding factor.

The place felt empty without her. He'd expected any day to move her in. The only reason he hadn't was because his future mother-in-law had frowned on them living together before they married. Sherrie was a dutiful daughter, whose mother heavily influenced her actions, even at twenty-five.

What do you mean future mother-in-law? That's over. Now you have nothing.

He felt sick. The dinner Keleeja had prepared earlier sat on his stomach like a rock. After all she'd done for him, he shouldn't make her life harder by throwing up on her floor. The least he could do was make it to the bathroom.

He stumbled in the general direction, but his legs gave out. His knees exploded with pain when he slammed down on them. Bile and dinner rose in his throat. He bit back a cry of agony, both physical and emotional. Good thing the girls were up in their room, preparing for bed. He wouldn't terrify them with his weakness.

"Colin?"

He thought he heard his name. For a second, it sounded like Sherrie. Blood roared through his head, making it hard to hear. Arms came around his shoulder. A hand rested on his chest. He realized he'd shut his eyes and bowed his head.

"Colin." She spoke directly in his ear, her lips brushing his skin. "It's okay. It's going to be okay."

He came to himself and looked at her.

"You should call Daniel."

"No. Not yet. It's better this way."

"What way? Torturing yourself? I don't understand."

"I should go."

"No, stay the night. I've already made up the bed in my mom's room. You can sleep there."

"You've done enough."

"You can tell me all about that in the morning. Come on. Help me get you up because you're a big guy. I can't throw my back out trying to lift you."

One minute hopelessness imprisoned him. The next, she made him want to laugh. Such an unusual woman. He had no idea why that fool Daniel let her get away and went back to disgusting Isabella.

"Thank you."

The muttered words were all he could say in response Keleeja's kindness and patience. After she led him into the spare bedroom, he sat on the side of the bed. A few minutes later, she returned with two white pills in the palm of her hand.

"Take these."

"I don't have a headache."

"They're sleeping pills. Don't worry. They're not

prescription. Autumn says they help her get extra shut eye when she needs it. She left them over here the last time she stayed the night. You look like you can use them."

He took the offering along with the glass of warm milk she handed him. "Milk? What am I one of your little sisters?"

"Sure. Drink up."

"I've never met a woman as bossy as you."

She grinned. "Goodnight, Colin. See you in the morning."

He shook his head, dropped back on the bed fully clothed, and tried to rest. A couple hours, and then he would leave to get back to his lonely miserable life.

CHAPTER 14

"Where is he?" Daniel stepped into the house without speaking and then realized what he'd done. "Sorry, Keleeja. Thank you for calling me. Is he alright? I can't believe he didn't phone me."

"He's upstairs asleep. I didn't want to let him know you were on your way until you got here in case he ran off."

Daniel's eyes widened. "Upstairs?"

"Yeah, he stayed the night in my mom's room. He was in a really bad place yesterday. I was worried he'd do something stupid. That's why I wouldn't let him out of my sight."

"That idiot." A flash of pain registered in his expression, and his jaw tightened. "He's mad at me. That's why he didn't call, but this is far more important than my issue. I'll take him off your hands."

"It's no trouble."

"Daniel!" Lola came flying down the stairs and jumped toward him.

Keleeja gasped. "Lola!"

Daniel's reflexes kicked in, and he caught the little girl easily. "Hey, pipsqueak. You remember me?"

"Yes. You ate chocolate cake and ice cream with us."

He nodded knowingly. "Ah, food-related memories. Understood."

Lola called up to her sisters. "Daniel's here." The other girls came charging down the stairs and gathered around him. Each, except for Tawney, vied for his attention and to be picked up the way he did Lola.

"Hang on, girls. I need to see my friend, okay? We'll talk later. Promise."

Keleeja gazed after him as he climbed the stairs. If possible, the man was more gorgeous than the last time she saw him. And the attraction was still there, stirring in her belly and giving her stupid thoughts.

She squelched the images in her head because he wasn't for her. He'd gone back to his wife. Even before then, he thought about the woman nonstop. Was she destined to meet men who weren't emotionally available?

Hold up, woman. What do you mean 'men'? Colin doesn't count.

She hurried into the kitchen, looking for something to distract her. Three of the girls sat at the table, munching cereal. Lola stood on her stool suspiciously close to the stove. "What are you doing, Lola?"

"Nothing." She dragged the last syllable of the word out.

"I know you're not trying to cook." Keleeja planted a hand on her hip. "How many times do we have to have this conversation?"

Lola blinked at her. "I wasn't trying to cook. I was getting cereal."

"Cereal is in the pantry."

"I was close to the pantry."

"You're near the stove."

"*Really* close."

Keleeja rolled her eyes toward the ceiling. It was no use. "Go get it."

Lola scampered into the pantry, hefting her stool with her. It was Sunday again, the day they made dinner together as a family. They planned the menu a couple days ago, and Autumn would arrive in an hour or so to help get started.

Keleeja wondered if anything new had come about from Autumn's camera drama. Come to think of it, she bet Colin as a private investigator would find the story interesting. Not that Keleeja would share her friend's secret, and Colin wasn't in the right headspace to appreciate hearing about it.

Steps on the stairs made her to check the fridge for what to offer the men. She doubted they wanted cereal. *Men.* What in the world were men doing in her house?

"Keleeja?" Daniel called out before he and Colin appeared. All day yesterday, Colin would materialize without saying a word, startling her. Getting him into conversation was like pulling teeth.

"Hey." She examined Colin in his rumpled clothing. "Sleep okay?"

He shrugged.

"Thanks again for looking out for him," Daniel told her.

To her surprise, he hugged her. She let him draw her close and then found an excuse to zip to the pantry. A package of Just Add Water pancake mix protected her from getting handsy with him.

"Stop thanking me. I only did what anyone would."

Colin eyed her hard but said nothing.

"We should get out of your hair. I know this is a special day," Daniel went on.

Keleeja's gaze wandered to his ring finger. He still didn't have it on. Maybe it was being cleaned or resized. She couldn't think why it would need to be resized. He hadn't gained an ounce in the last few months.

"Why is it a special day?" Colin wondered aloud. "Someone's birthday?"

"Mine," Tawney said breathless.

"Not yet." Keleeja shook her head. "Her birthday isn't until week after next. Daniel means it's Sunday. On Sunday, we have family dinners, which we cook together. My friend Autumn comes over, and we make a big production of it."

Colin didn't respond.

"You guys are welcome to have breakfast here," she offered. "We don't get started cooking for about an hour or more. The girls usually eat cereal for breakfast and a piece of fruit or something later, until we're done with dinner."

As she spoke, the doorbell rang. A second later, Autumn called out. "Hey! Anybody home?"

"In the kitchen," Keleeja shouted back.

"Who's in my spot? I had to park down the block. Looks like your neighbors are having the world over for the weekend aga—"

Autumn stopped speaking when she walked into the kitchen. Her curious gaze flicked from Colin to Daniel, recognized him with a small light of displeasure, and then flicked back to Colin again. Her interest peaked, and she smiled at him.

"Hello, I'm Autumn. You are?" No shyness there when walking into a crowded room.

Keleeja thought Colin would ignore her, but he introduced himself. "Colin Voss. Friend of Keleeja's. I stayed the night."

Autumn let out a choked sound, her eyes rounding.

"Someone is feeling better after a good night's sleep." Daniel smacked the back of a hand against his buddy's arm. "You're joking around."

"It's true."

Autumn gasped. "Maybe we need to take this conversation into another room!"

All four girls watched them from the table.

Keleeja gestured for them to get back to their food, and they obeyed. Lola took her time turning around. "There's nothing to discuss. Colin is being ridiculous."

"Colin was sick," Lola volunteered. "We took care of him, Autumn."

"You did?" Autumn zipped over to give Lola a kiss on the top of her head. She followed up with smooches for each of the girls. "That's sweet of you. What did you do to take care of him?"

Tawney demonstrated wit beyond her years. "We let him fold the laundry."

Autumn laughed.

"And we played Uno with him so he could be happy," Lily added. "I think his stomach was hurting. Uno makes me feel better when my stomach hurts."

Autumn nodded. "Good idea."

When Keleeja turned back to the men after listening to this conversation, she found a spark of amusement in both men's eyes. That was the way it always was. The girls kept her entertained.

"Again," she said, "the offer of breakfast stands. I don't mind. I plan to spend all morning in here anyway."

"Since you have the pancake mix out..." Daniel grinned. "I came over right after you called, so I skipped breakfast. You don't mind, do you, Colin? Good."

Colin frowned at not being given a real choice, but he grabbed a seat next to Lola at the table.

Keleeja started on a pan of sausage and brought out eggs from the fridge. "Girls, when you're done, put your bowls in the sink. Tawney, wipe the table, please."

The kitchen became a buzz of activity. The girls were reluctant to leave in case they missed anything. Keleeja dared not ask Autumn about work in front of the others, so she let Autumn and Daniel carry the conversation. Daniel seemed determined to keep it moving and tried to get Colin involved. Colin sat like a silent grumpy lump.

Keleeja checked the pantry for another bottle of syrup, and Daniel joined her. His scent filled the small space, tantalizing her nostrils and her senses. She tried to keep her head on straight, but it wasn't easy given his nearness.

"I'm sorry to dump all this one you," he commented. "But thank you for keeping him going yesterday."

"It's no trouble. How are you, Daniel?"

"Not as good as I'd like. It hurts me to see him like this. But I know he'll bounce back in no time. That's Colin. He's not the down in the dumps kind of man, even if he's feeling crushed at the moment."

She nodded. "I meant…"

"Ah." He ran a hand over his face, and the air in the pantry thickened with tension. "He told you, huh? That I went back."

"That's none of my business. I wasn't asking…" Wasn't she though? His going back to his ex-wife ticked her off and hurt at the same time, which was stupid considering they weren't even seeing each other. They agreed last time they were together that they weren't meant to be.

"I was stupid." Daniel rubbed his bare ring finger.

She waited for him to explain.

"Isabella and I are technically together, but I've been telling her we're done. It's not going to work out. She's too selfish. The only positive thing I can say about her is—"

"I've got to get this syrup out to the others." Keleeja left him standing there.

"Wait, I'm sorry, Keleeja." He grabbed her arm to keep her from leaving the pantry.

"Your personal life is none of my business." She shook his hold off and returned to preparing breakfast.

At the table, Keleeja started making plates for the adults. Colin stole a sausage link and munched it down. Lola's eyes rounded. She almost drooled on his arm as she stood beside him. He grabbed another link and held it out to her.

Her face lit up. "Thanks, Colin."

"I want one!" a cacophony rose among the others. Colin fed all the girls sausage.

Autumn laughed. "I know somebody they can twist around their little fingers."

"Now I've got to make more," Keleeja complained.

"You weren't going to give them food?"

"They ate breakfast, and we usually eat a huge meal later when they stuff themselves to the gills."

"Not to mention all the begging for snacks," Autumn added. "Don't let them fool you, Colin. Our little sweet peas aren't starving. Those puppy dog eyes are just for you."

Keleeja laughed. She knew Autumn spoke the truth. The girls knew how cute they were and how to use that cuteness to get what they wanted. Sometimes Keleeja couldn't resist it, but she tried to be stern with them when they needed it.

After breakfast, Colin started clearing the table. Daniel watched him, curiosity in his eyes. He looked from his friend to Keleeja and back again. She pretended not to notice. When the kitchen was clean, Daniel excused himself to use the facilities.

"Autumn, can we watch the princess movie again?" Lily asked.

"Yay, the princess movie," the other girls echoed.

Autumn laughed. "We've only seen it fifty-five million times. But okay. Come on. Keleeja, we're not ready yet, right?"

"A little over an hour I think."

"Cool."

Keleeja was left alone with Colin. He stood before the dishwasher as it rumbled through its cycle.

She touched his arm. "Okay?"

"I don't need your babying."

"I know. Jeez, you're annoying."

A ghost of a smile touched his lips, and she noticed the shape of them and the stubble on his jaw. He was handsome in a boy-next-door kind of way, so big and comfortable with his size. His fiancée was probably a beautiful woman, who was right for him. All of a sudden, she desperately wished all the hurt and disappointment and everything negative could be put behind all of them.

He touched her cheek, startling her from her thoughts, and her eyes widened. His thumb brushed her skin, and the tingle throughout her system shocked her.

"W-what are you doing, Colin?"

He blinked and came to himself then stepped back. "Sorry."

"Don't worry about it. No big deal."

"I'm going now."

She nodded.

"Thanks for making me feel better by making me fold clothes."

She laughed. "Isn't she a trip?"

"All of them are. You're lucky."

"I am. Blessed. You will be too. I know it. I can see you're a good person."

A real smile this time. "How can you? I've been grouchy and difficult."

"When you can laugh and smile again, come see me and show me the real you."

"Deal."

It was just words. She didn't mean for him to take her seriously. Not that it mattered. He and Daniel would go on with their lives, and the chance encounter with Colin wouldn't repeat itself. They lived in too big a city for that to happen twice. Three times, if one included the downtown ice cream thing.

She saw them both off a short while later and continued with her family's Sunday tradition.

CHAPTER 15

"So? Has he called?"

Keleeja scraped a row of dull white shirts aside to get to the lime-colored one. Her instincts proved to be right. It was a definite maybe. The little lemon man with scrawny legs and arms was cute. Lara would love it, and it was her size.

"Did who call?" She added the cost of the shirt to her mental running total. Yeah, she could do one more.

She and Autumn had gone shopping at the thrift store while the girls were in daycare. The free time was a rare treat, yet Keleeja still ended up doing something for the girls. They needed a few new things, so it couldn't be avoided.

Autumn pursed her lips. "You know who I mean. Daniel. Or heck, did Colin? Either one would be fine."

"You know he just lost his fiancée, right? The man is grieving. Plus, there was never anything there. I only met him through Daniel."

"He's single. He's male. He's gorgeous as I don't

114

know what." Autumn's forehead creased. "Come to think of it, you've got a real knack for meeting good-looking guys. We need to go out so you can be my wing man and I can find a hottie."

Keleeja snorted. "It was a fluke. Then again, maybe cute guys flock together. I've never noticed."

"Me either. It's something to think about."

"To answer your question, Colin texted."

"I knew it!"

"So did Daniel."

"Oh, choices. Nice."

Keleeja rolled her eyes. "Neither is serious. Colin likes how I take his mind off his broken heart. Daniel… I don't know what his deal is, but I'm not giving him a chance. As far as I know he's still with his ex. When I think about the two of them, I feel like I draw the emotionally unavailable men. That stinks."

"Don't think of it like that."

"How can I not?"

When her friend moved to another aisle, Keleeja pulled her phone out to look at the messages again. It had only been a week, and here she'd heard from both of them. She pulled up the message from Colin first and snickered.

"I folded them."

He'd sent a picture of a pile of t-shirts on the bed, and all were neatly folded. What a nut. He thought that was something to celebrate. She supposed it was since he'd never folded anything before he came to her house. The amusing part was remembering that

Tawney joked about making him feel better with folding the laundry.

Keleeja had sent a laughing emoji along with a thumbs up in response and didn't hear from Colin again. As for Daniel's text...

"I want to take you to dinner again, just us this time."

She didn't answer because she didn't know what to say. Not to mention the fact that he ticked her off because he didn't say whether his ex moved out. Then again, she doubted he would ask her for a date while still with his wife.

When she didn't respond, he didn't contact her again. That was a day ago. Yet, her mind stayed on the two men.

"You should call one of them and ask him out."

"Autumn, why are you always trying to set me up?"

"Because if I can't find love, you can, and I can live vicariously through you. We're not getting any younger."

"Yeah, I'm hurtling toward thirty, and I don't like it." Keleeja sighed.

They made their purchases and then went to find a restaurant to have lunch.

"So?" Keleeja popped a fry into her mouth. The greasy goodness did her mood good. "What's happening with your boss? Catch him in the act yet? Or did you come to your senses and remove the camera?"

Autumn chose pizza for lunch, and she shook enough red pepper flakes on it to burn a hole in her tongue. "The camera stays. What I need is someone I can trust to be the bait. That way, the film will be admissible in court."

"Say what?"

"You know how they say one of the parties has to be aware of the recording?"

"Um, I think so. Maybe? Also, isn't that from TV? We have zero idea if that stuff is legal."

"It must be. At least, I hope it is. I haven't had the chance to research it yet."

"Autumn."

"Don't get onto me, Lee." She banged a fist on the table. "I've got to get Jeff. I'm determined to."

"For revenge?"

"For womankind."

Keleeja gave up. "Well, I didn't suggest this before because it was too soon. Maybe he's back to work. I don't know, but it's worth a shot."

"You're talking in code, my friend."

Keleeja laughed. "I'm talking about Colin. He's a private investigator. He'll probably know the legal stuff about recording and all that."

Autumn perked up. "Perfect! Call him."

"I thought you would remind me I have to keep your secret."

Autumn took a huge bite of her pizza and spoke around the food in her mouth. "You can say you're asking for a friend who's not Autumn and ask his advice."

"So you've decided you're taking this to the police?"

She squared her shoulders. "I've been thinking about it. If I'm not willing to go all the way with this, then why do I think I'm the better candidate for the promotion?"

"I doubt one has to do with the other."

"Regardless. I'm prepared to see it through."

"Okay, I'll call Colin."

"Now?" Autumn looked hopeful.

Keleeja sighed. "Fine." She dialed him and was surprised when he answered on the first ring.

"Keleeja."

"Hey, Colin. How are you?"

"Better. I wanted to thank you for being there. I don't know if I would have done something stupid, but it got dicey there the first day."

"I hear you. I'm glad you're doing better. I have a favor to ask."

"Anything."

His voice rumbled so pleasantly, and he sounded friendlier. She was curious to know him when he wasn't in the depths of despair. Was he as sweet as Daniel? Sweeter? He didn't seem to be that type, but who knew.

"I wanted to pick your brain on the legalities of something. You might know because of your work in private investigations and such. Do you think you'd be up for a talk about it?"

"We can go to dinner tonight and discuss it."

Her jaw dropped. Wait, he wasn't asking her out on a date. He was being accommodating because she helped him out. He wanted to return the favor in some small way.

"Hang on. I have to ask Autumn is she can sit with the kids."

"Yes!" Autumn shouted.

Several heads turned in their direction, and Autumn blushed. She covered her mouth, eyes shining with amusement and excitement. The woman was crazy.

"I guess you heard that, Colin? The nutball says she'll watch the girls."

"Then I'll pick you up at six."

"Thanks."

ow! One week brought an amazing change in Colin. He probably didn't gain that much weight, but he'd certainly stopped skipping meals. The bags under his eyes were gone, and his skin had taken on a more natural color. He'd gotten a haircut, and his clothes looked fresh. In fact, he smelled heavenly when he surprised her with a hug.

Something deep inside stirred to feel his strong arms around her and the solid wall of his chest. When they drew apart, she caught her breath at his nearness. He offered a slight smile with only a bit of sadness reflected in his silver eyes. She couldn't believe the quake that racked her body.

Get it together, Keleeja. This isn't a date, and you sure as heck aren't interested in him.

She gave herself some slack. After all, she was a little lonely for male companionship, and Colin was gorgeous. Why wouldn't she respond physically to him? Better to enjoy the view and not sweat it.

"You look amazing," she admitted. "Night and day."

He chuckled. "Meaning I looked like the walking dead the last time you saw me?"

"Yup."

"You don't bite your tongue."

"But I'm not mean."

He agreed. "I like that about you."

She warmed at his words and perused the menu. Her stomach growled. She'd eaten very little at lunchtime because of nerves and excitement at seeing him again. Maybe they could be friends and dinner out could be an occasional occurrence. She'd enjoy that since she didn't have many friends. Autumn was pretty much it because the girls kept her busy. A social life was nonexistent.

"Is the food good here? This place is a little out of my price range."

"I'm picking up the tab, so don't worry about that."

She grinned. "I wasn't. I'm modern but not *that* modern. I'm glad to let you get the bill."

He chuckled again. She liked his laugh.

"Yes, the food's great. This is my favorite restaurant. Daniel and I happened to go to school with the owner. If he ever let the place go, he'd hear it from one of us."

"Wow, another one of you with your own business. I'm so jealous."

"Don't be. Just start your own."

"Uh-huh. Cause it's so easy."

"I didn't say it's easy. Just doable."

They ordered drinks and food. Keleeja chose riga-toni with braised pork, and Colin nodded approval. When the food arrived, she made sure he ate his choice. From the look of it, she had nothing to worry about. He wolfed his food down like any other man. This time, he didn't have that vacant dullness in his eyes, and his moves weren't mechanical. His appetite had returned.

When they were almost done with the meal, she relaxed enough to discuss why she called him. "So I have this friend."

"Autumn?"

"No. Um, someone else." She didn't feel comfortable lying, but she and Autumn agreed to keep her name out of the conversation. Colin would need details about the situation, and she didn't want to implicate her friend in something illegal.

"Go on."

She explained everything about Autumn's boss and what he was rumored to be up to. Colin frowned. "Is it just rumors?"

"She hasn't come out and said anything specific—which worries me—but I trust that she has valid reasons for suspecting him. And there were others who wanted to do something about him, but they chickened out at the last minute."

"You want to know what her options are?"

She swallowed. "There's more. See, she's placed a video camera in his office."

His eyes widened.

"My friend wants to know if she gets him on video

doing what he does, can she take it to the police, or will it be accepted in court? Will she get into trouble for recording him? We heard there's a law protecting her in some way. Do you know anything about it?"

He wiped his mouth, a thoughtful look in his eyes. "I'm not an expert in law."

Disappointment washed over her.

"The law I know about differs from state to state. Here, we have one-party-consent protection. That's where one person involved in a conversation consents to be recorded, or they make the recording themselves. But that has to do with audio."

"What about video?"

"I'm not sure. However, there's another complication."

Her stomach knotted.

"Well, one or two. First, she might get away with a video recording in a public location, where there isn't any expectation of privacy. But you're saying she hid the camera in this guy's office. That's not a public place. There's also the company policy."

"Company policy?"

"It's likely written in the company's policy manual that no recordings are allowed without permission. Your friend could be terminated if the brass finds out about the recording. It's also a possible violation of this guy's privacy, and he could file a civil suit against her."

"Oh no! Then it's hopeless. I should tell her to remove the camera as soon as possible."

"Is this guy really the piece of trash she thinks he is?"

"Like I said, she believes so."

"Then she can get him somewhere else, away from the company, in a way that doesn't risk the loss of her job."

"I don't know. Sounds risky and dangerous all the same. I want her safe."

"I can come up with a plan and execute it, all without her direct involvement."

She gasped. "Really, Colin? That would be so fantastic, but it can't get in the way of your regular work. I don't know what your fee is, but I'm sure she'll pay it if it's reasonable."

"No charge. I'm doing this for a friend."

She liked him thinking of her as a friend. "Thanks."

"And it won't interfere with my work. I'm taking on as much as possible for a while."

She understood. He wanted to stay busy until his pain eased. "You're so sweet. We appreciate it."

"Give me Autumn's number, and tell her I'll give her a call in a couple days when I've worked out the preliminaries of my plan. Tell her to remove the camera ASAP."

"Autumn?"

He flicked an eyebrow skyward. "Come on, Keleeja. I wouldn't be any good at my job if I couldn't tell when a woman like you was lying."

"A woman like me?" She wasn't sure if she should be offended.

"An open and honest one. Your face is as expressive as any I've ever seen."

"Well I never," she joked, and they both laughed.

He could laugh again. That was nice. Maybe it didn't go as deep as before, but it would. She had hope he would bounce back from the tragedy he suffered. And some woman, whoever she was, would be lucky to have him. He was a good guy. Funny how hidden that fact was when she first met him.

Not now though. A year or two?

She suppressed the speculation. It had nothing to do with her. Dang it. She liked to be honest with herself, and she had to admit she really liked him. On the other hand, it was easy to start liking a guy who was cute and—there. She hated unnecessary feelings rising up and circumstances dictating them.

"So now that that business is over, talk to me," he urged.

He surprised her. "You want to talk?"

"I was a surly mess last time you saw me."

"And the time before that."

He chuckled. "I would have said something awful if I opened my mouth too much."

"You were a bit rough a few times."

"I'm sorry."

"Don't worry about it. We can start over and be great friends."

"Agreed. I liked how you spoke to me when you found me in that parking lot."

She thought back and groaned. "I was so bossy. I'm not like that usually. I promise."

"Why do I doubt that?"

"Hey!"

"No, I needed the kick in the pants and the help.

Sherrie… Never mind. You don't want to hear about her. Tell me about your sisters. How are they? Crying for me?"

"Yeah right." She laughed. "But Lola did ask when you were coming over to play again. Somehow, she's gotten the impression you're *her* playmate."

"Easy to understand. I lost at Uno so gracefully. She's looking trounce me a few more times."

"I bet she is. That girl. But no, don't resist talking about your fiancée on my account. We're friends. If you need to talk about her, do it. I don't mind."

He shook his head stubbornly. "My entire family invaded my house a couple days after I left your place. Daniel called them. I've been talking nonstop about her since then. I finally got my mom to stop calling every hour to check on me. That was after I evicted her and told her to go home."

"Colin. She's worried about you."

"I know, but I'm a very independent man. I don't like being fussed over."

"I fussed over you when you were at my house."

"No. You forced me to stay occupied. That's different. Mom wants to hover and baby me. It drives me nuts."

"It sounds like you guys are really close. I love that."

He studied her face for a few silent moments. "I can find her for you."

She gasped. "My mom? How will that help? The fact that she left at all is too much, and if she doesn't want to be near us, then it's her loss."

"It hurts you."

"Yeah, but I'm used to her being gone now. As far as I'm concerned, it's just me, the girls, and Autumn. We'll be fine without her. So while I appreciate your offer, it's not necessary. Even when I was little, I couldn't really depend on her."

He nodded understanding.

"I had to grow up fast and figure things out for myself. My mom has always been more interested in her next boyfriend. Ugh, let's change the subject. I'm making myself mad. Tell me more about your family."

"Where to start? They've crowded me so much over the years, I sometimes wish they'd go on a trip for a year."

She snorted. "You're kidding?"

"Yes. Not about the crowding. I end up at my parents' place on holidays, bringing gifts for my nieces and nephews."

"So that's why you weren't intimidated with my sisters."

He glared.

"Oh right. No one intimidates Colin Voss."

"Should they?"

"No. You're hilarious. So are you going to add to the size of your family some day?"

His countenance darkened, and she rushed to apologize.

"I'm so sorry. I forgot about…"

He sat back in his seat and sighed. "I dated a lot. Some were special. None stood out to me as much as Sherrie. Something about her—she treated me like—" He gritted his teeth together. She waited in silence, knowing he needed this, even though he resisted talking about her up until now.

He shared all about the woman with the great legs and sweet smile. The way she loved him, that's what drew him to her. Open and honest, always upbeat, and loving life. Keleeja's heart ached for Colin because it sounded like Sherrie was fresh air to his routine existence of nonstop investigations.

"I committed to her when I didn't think twice about it before. And I put up with her mom because of her."

"Was her mom so bad?"

"Smothering."

"Yikes. There's that word again."

"Yeah. She smothered her daughter and demanded from me on her daughter's behalf. I took it in stride for Sherrie. But now she's gone."

Keleeja reached for his hand and squeezed it. He surprised her, curling strong fingers around hers. "I'm so sorry, Colin. I wish I had the power to give her back to you."

"You," he said.

"Me what?"

"Nothing." He pulled away and grabbed the check the waiter left on the table. "Come on. Let's get out of here."

"Of course."

She felt like she overstepped in some way. At first they flowed along like friends, and now it felt like he withdrew. Maybe she pushed him too hard to talk about his fiancée. He might not have been ready. Who was she to decide he needed it?

"I'll call Autumn soon. Don't worry, okay?" The distance she felt disappeared, and he was the man she first saw when they walked into the restaurant. "I always get my prey."

"Yikes. Prey?"

"Yeah. *Always.* Just a matter of time."

CHAPTER 17

"This is a mistake, Autumn."

"No, it's not." Her friend stepped up behind her and tucked a stray lock of hair behind Keleeja's ear. "You look fabulous, and he's going to go gaga over you."

"Hello? He's just lost the love of his life, and it's only been a month since then. There's no way in the world he'll go 'gaga' over me. And I shouldn't be going out on an official date with him either. I'm just asking for heartbreak."

"You're asking for some male companionship—and maybe more later."

"Autumn."

"What? You're human, aren't you? Just because you have little sisters to raise doesn't mean you don't want a man's touch. I know I do. But maybe things are changing in that arena."

"What do you mean?"

"Never mind." Autumn spun her toward the

bedroom door and gave her a little push. "Don't count Colin out. Everybody says the person they love is the love of their life. Then they break up and find someone new. Then *they're* the one. Bah!"

"That argument inspires zero confidence."

"Would you just have fun? He's yummy good looking. He laughs at your jokes, and he's helping me get that loser Jeff. What more could you ask for?"

Keleeja laughed. "I have the feeling you want me to keep him smiling long enough to get your situation dealt with."

"It couldn't hurt. If you don't make him laugh, he'll sit in his house and mope. He needs you."

"He doesn't need me. He has Daniel."

"Who was a great disappointment."

"He called me yesterday."

"What? That man doesn't give up. Was his wife in the background?"

"No, he said she moved out—again."

"Ugh."

"Yeah. But…"

"No, Lee. He's a jerk for leading you on and then running back to his wife."

"But he's a little more available than Colin. Don't you think?"

Autumn's shoulders slumped a bit. "Maybe both need to go. But what other prospects do you have?"

"I thought the same thing." Keleeja ran back to the mirror to get one last look at herself. She wore a black sleeveless dress, nothing fancy but it complemented her curves. She looked decent, kind of cute.

The dress fit snugly but not slutlike against her figure.

She and Colin spoke many times over the phone and through texts. They had become good friends, and a few nights ago, he asked her out on a date. She'd said yes right away, but she wondered if that was the wrong decision. Colin might be looking for someone to distract him from his pain. He had no genuine interest in her. How could he under the circumstances?

But I still said yes, and here we are.

She rubbed the sudden chill bumps rising on her arms. What if she fell in love with him, and he tore her heart out? She'd fallen for a guy a few years ago, and he cheated. The experience devastated her, especially since she didn't get many opportunities for dating—certainly not since her mom left.

It's just fun. That's it. He's a friend, nothing more. Don't fall, Keleeja.

The doorbell rang.

"Crud, he's early," she moaned.

"Eager," Autumn agreed. She ran out of the room, and Keleeja took her time heading downstairs. Her legs felt wobbly, and her throat dried. She held on for dear life to the banister and prayed she'd keep her head on straight.

At the bottom of the stairs, Autumn opened the door, and there he was. Tall, gorgeous, and even though she was still halfway up the steps, she could swear she breathed in his delicious scent. Good golly how was she supposed to cope with this?

Silver eyes assessed her coolly. She was reminded of

his attitude when she first met him and cringed against it a little. Then he smiled and transformed.

"Wow, you look great." He stepped into the house, and when she reached him, he laid gentle big hands at her waist and drew her forward. She gasped when he leaned in and kissed her cheek.

It's just your cheek, Keleeja. Get ahold of yourself.

He breathed in and whispered. "Mm, smell nice too."

She smacked his hands and stepped back. "Would you stop?"

He looked past her. "Where are the girls? I thought I'd say hi."

"Asleep. They go to bed at eight, and we're getting a late start."

He frowned. "Is it okay? You're not too tired? That meeting was the only time I could arrange, and this guy is hard to pin down."

"Don't worry about it. I'm good. I had a snack earlier."

"Are you always so understanding?"

"No, so don't push it."

He laughed, and behind him Autumn mouthed "See? You make him laugh."

Keleeja almost rolled her eyes but resisted. "We better get moving, or I might fall asleep in my dinner. Then again, I can't guarantee I won't."

When Colin pulled into a hotel parking lot and started to get out of the car, Keleeja grabbed his arm to stop him.

"Whoa, what do you think we're doing tonight? I

never agreed to sleep with you, and certainly not at a hotel. What kind of woman do you think I am?" Anger surged in her veins. She'd thought Colin was different, but he went and assumed asking her out equaled sleeping with him? He was mistaken if he thought she was a weak-minded, low self-esteem woman.

"Easy. It's not what you think."

"Why don't you explain it to me?"

He grinned at her. Even in the car's dim lighting, she could tell she amused him. Autumn was right. The bum was already having a good time. She served to distract him easily enough, but that's not what she wanted.

"Autumn's boss is in there."

Her jaw dropped. "What? But you said you were still setting it up."

"He took the bait faster than I expected. A real sleaze. I thought the girl I got to tempt him would have to work harder. Turns out she was just his type."

"Wait, what girl? You didn't tell Autumn all this."

"I wanted to keep the details to myself until everything was in place. Autumn is… She's a smart woman but…"

Keleeja knew what he was getting at. "She gets a little too excited. You were worried she would say something to someone and blow the whole thing. Forget about that. What girl are you talking about?"

"I should have said woman. I hired someone to go through a temp agency and get placed at Autumn's company. She's an actress/waitress I use sometimes for my cases, and she's good at what she does."

"What does she do?"

"Why don't we talk on the way so we don't miss the main event?"

"This is why you asked me out?"

He glanced at her. "You said you wanted to get involved."

"I said I wanted to know more about what you do, especially when it comes to Autumn."

Disappointment racked her system. She'd dressed up for this fool, spent hours fussing over her hair to get it right. The date turned out to be a job. This was the same bullcrap Daniel pulled on their first date, taking her to see his depressed friend. What in the heck was up with these men?

Or was it her? She didn't instill desire in them, didn't cause them to see her as a woman. Come to think of it, Colin never said he dated a Black woman. Maybe it wasn't even a thing in his mind, so he didn't know he tempted her. What an idiot she was.

She hardly listened as he explained his plan.

"Zoe played the sweet little innocent, eager to please the boss, and he swooped in like a shark on the attack. He told her he had an important meeting at this hotel and that he needs her assistance."

"So he plans to proposition her sometime tonight?"

"No, he plans to get what he wants, by any means necessary."

Keleeja stopped walking. "What?"

"I've interviewed a couple of the women who used to work for him. He's not just using his position to get them to let him have his way."

She felt sick. "Autumn. He didn't—"

"No. As far as I could tell it never happened with Autumn. She also denies it. Plus she's not his type. That's why she didn't get the promotion."

Keleeja nodded. "She's the most wonderful person you could ever meet, but yeah, she's plump. She wouldn't be his type."

"I meant her intelligence and assertive nature. Those would be a real turn off to a guy like him. He wants to manipulate women and hurt them. That stops tonight."

On one hand, Keleeja admired Colin for helping her friend so quickly while keeping it all legal. However, with him letting her think they were going on an actual date and instead bringing her to the shakedown of Autumn's boss, she choked on regret. At the same time, she couldn't complain. He was doing them a favor, one he didn't owe them.

He led her into the hotel's restaurant. "Sit tight at the bar while I go assess the situation."

"Sure."

He left, and she ordered a sparkling water, feeling sorry for herself. Down the bar, a man caught her eye and raised his glass. She offered him a half smile. Annoyance and dejection hit so strongly she didn't bother to check whether the guy was cute.

Her cell phone dinged.

"Up for a chat?"

Daniel. So he didn't know she was out on a "date" with his friend. Impulse made her phone him. "Hey, Daniel. How's it going?"

"Good. Did you get my text the other day?"

"Yes."

He chuckled. "Not going to give an excuse for ignoring me, huh?"

"Better than lying."

"Ouch. You sound like you're in a bad mood. Should I talk to you later?"

"I'm out on a date actually."

"Who's stealing you from me?"

"Please." She rolled her eyes. "Colin went to take care of something real quick."

She had no idea why she would even bring Colin up. Playing games. It wasn't like her, but she wasn't immune to it either. She stuffed the shame down.

"Keleeja," Daniel growled. "Why are you out with him?"

"Whoa. Excuse me?"

"He's never going to get serious about you. He's just lost his fiancée, or did you forget?"

He echoed her own worries.

"And you just broke up for the fiftieth time with your wife. Are you saying you're better?"

"I'm sorry." The anger disappeared in a heartbeat like it always did. "I have no right to dictate to you who you should and shouldn't date. I like you—a lot. And I don't want to see you get hurt."

"I appreciate that."

"But I wouldn't be a good friend if I didn't warn you."

"Thanks for the heads-up."

"You're still mad at me."

"Not really."

"Just out of curiosity, where did he take you?"

She was tempted to mention the hotel. Daniel would really blow a gasket. She bit back a laugh thinking about it and looked around. "Nice swanky place. Upscale from the looks of it."

"I'll take you wherever you'd like to go."

"Is this a competition? I'm not interested in being the prize, and I'm definitely not the kind of woman who is okay coming between friends. Or is that something you two do all the time?"

"No, not since we were in high school, but it was no contest."

"Meaning you won?"

He laughed. "How about Tuesday night?"

"Tuesday?"

"Dinner with me, and a movie if you like."

She thought of the last movie she went to see, a children's one. The kids were too young at the time and couldn't keep still or quiet. She hadn't tried again since. Of course, Daniel tempted her.

Hesitation stirred in her. She looked up to see Colin heading back into the bar. Feelings of anger and attraction stirred inside. He didn't take her seriously as a date. Even if he did want to help Autumn on her behalf, he knew what she would think when he asked her out. It was insensitive to let her think it was about her and not the case. She didn't want to cut him anymore slack because of his loss.

"Okay. That's fine. Call me tomorrow, and we can work out the details."

She ended the call as Colin walked up. Colin's brow creased with curiosity. "Did I hear you say Daniel?"

"How did it go? Is he going for it?"

"Should be. I came down to get you. We have the room next to the one he's using, and I set her up with a recording device. We can listen in."

"Maybe Autumn should have been here. She would love to see the takedown for herself."

"Probably."

"And you could have skipped the middleman —*woman*. This is about her and not me after all."

He frowned. "Are you angry for some reason? What did Daniel say to make you mad?"

She snorted and walked past him. "Come on. Let's get this show on the road so I can get back to my family."

CHAPTER 18

Colin knew why Keleeja was angry. He'd known from the beginning he was being a fool—and a jerk. She deserved better treatment. What's more, she had become one of his closest friends in the short time he'd known her.

They spoke often, laughed together. He would be deaf, dumb, and blind not to see what an amazing and beautiful woman she was. And he'd be an idiot if he wasn't attracted to her. The problem was Sherrie looming in his memory, reminding him of how much he had loved her.

He felt like he was cheating to care about Keleeja, to want Keleeja. So when temptation came over him to ask Keleeja to dinner and she accepted, he later made sure to make the date about business. In trying to protect himself, he hurt her. That was unacceptable and cowardly.

In the hotel room, with his equipment set up to listen and record Zoe's encounter with Jeff, his usual excitement in what he did for a living faded. Keleeja sat at the small round table, legs crossed and holding her purse on her lap like a protection device. The big brown eyes stared off in the distance, and her mouth compressed into a straight line. She hadn't spoken to him since they stepped onto the elevator to come up to the room.

He swallowed a sigh and removed the plug from the headphones so Keleeja could hear what he heard.

"I don't know about this, Mr. Slathers. I-I-I have a boyfriend, and you're married. Plus…"

"Zoe, easy. This isn't a big deal. Everyone does it. In fact, they expect it. You want the job permanently, don't you?"

"Yes, but this way? It's not what I thought I was getting into. You said we were coming to this hotel to work."

"Come on, Zoe. You know the drill."

"I don't."

Zoe spoke a little more firmly with him. Colin heard a spark of anger and hoped she could hang on a bit longer. He didn't blame her for probably wanting to kick him where it hurt most and walk out of there. Colin's muscles tensed, ready to come to her rescue when the time came.

Keleeja surged to her feet and tossed her purse on the table. She paced, eyes shooting fire at what she heard. Her hands bunched into fists at her sides. He imagined she wanted to break something over Jeff's head at that moment.

"Don't waste your time or mine, Zoe. You know what I want."

"What do you want?"

Colin ground his teeth. Still too forceful. She was losing it. He thought about alternatives to tonight if things went wrong.

"I want you. Take off your clothes and get on the bed."

Keleeja's mouth fell open. She stared hard at Colin.

"It's okay," he whispered. "She'll be okay. I promise."

She frowned at him and turned away, wrapping her arms around herself. He should have realized before now that what was common to him in his line of work would be shocking and traumatizing to Keleeja. Bringing her on the job was almost a punishment for making him want to be with her. It wasn't right, and he was ashamed of himself. He would find a way to make it up to her.

Or I could get out of her life, so I won't hurt her again.

The thought bothered him. He liked her more than he could explain, even to himself. She was a lot like Sherrie and vastly different at the same time. Honest and sweet like Sherrie but with a strength Sherrie couldn't imagine, Keleeja drew him closer, made him curious, amused him.

It's not realistic. There's no way she could be someone important to me so soon. I must be compensating for the loss.

"Colin!" Keleeja dug her nails in his arm, eyes wide with fear.

He shook himself to attention and realized that the situation had come to a head with Jeff. "Wait here."

"No way! I'm going in there with you!"

She shoved past him into the room next door. The couple lay on the bed, Jeff trying to pin Zoe down. She had a hold of his hair and tried to scream around a heavy hand over her mouth.

"Get your hands off of her, you disgusting piece of garbage," Keleeja shouted.

She launched herself at the bed. Colin grabbed her arm to pull her back and moved ahead of her. In two seconds he had Jeff by the collar and pulled his phone out of his pocket.

"Keleeja? What are you doing here? And who are you? This is a private room. I'm—"

"You're going to jail. That's what you're doing." Keleeja hugged Zoe and helped her to sit up. "Are you okay. Come on. Let's go next door so you can take a minute to catch your breath."

That's what she did, Colin thought. She looked after others, freely gave her support. His response to her character wasn't anything more than gratitude in a time of need. With half his thoughts still on Keleeja after she and Zoe went next door, he wrapped things up with Jeff and the police when they arrived.

"This is entrapment," Jeff complained. "I want to speak with my lawyer. You're not going to get away with this. I don't know who you think you are, but *I'm* a big deal. A lot of people owe me favors."

Colin got up in his face, ignoring the officer's hand and warning to back off. "You're *nothing*, and you're not the only one with connections."

A vein bulged in the older man's forehead, making his receding hairline more pronounced. "It's my word against hers. She tried to seduce me and changed her mind. I was just trying to startle her into realizing you don't play with a man's desires."

"Oh, is that all?" Colin handed over the disk with the recording on it to the officer. "This will prove what his intentions were. I'll also drop by the station in the morning with recorded statements and signed affidavits of two others he's done this to."

The blood drained from Jeff's face. Reality about his situation hit, and he went mute. Colin left the rest to the police and returned to the room next door. He found Keleeja alone.

"Where's Zoe?"

"She said all she wanted to do was go home and shower."

"She'll need to give the police a statement."

"That can wait, can't it? I don't blame her for wanting to get out of here. I'm desperate to myself."

He stood in front of her and rubbed her arms. "I'm sorry. I shouldn't have brought you here. It was a bad decision on my part and…"

He froze, not wanting to admit the truth to her but knowing he should. It was the least he could do to begin to make it up to her for the poor treatment.

"Honestly, I wanted to do something that would put a little distance between us because I'm attracted to you, and it didn't feel right."

She said nothing. He couldn't see her face since she'd lowered her head.

"I'm sorry. You deserve better. Let me make it up to you."

The room echoed with silence.

"Keleeja?"

She looked up at him at last. There was that fire in her eyes and determined set to her jaw. "No."

He widened his eyes. "Huh?"

"I said no thank you. I'm going home. Please take me now, or I can call a taxi."

"It doesn't have to be tonight."

"Again, no thank you. I'm good." Her calm and sensible tone grated. "So are you taking me home or am I calling a taxi?"

He sighed. "I'll take you."

When they reached his car, he couldn't help asking the question that tramped through his head.

"Were you making a date with Daniel earlier?"

"That's none of your business."

"Keleeja. I know you're mad at me, and if you let me explain—"

"You already told me your reasoning. I get it. You feel guilty wanting me. That's fine. I already knew you weren't ready. I'm not going to sit around waiting or hoping you will be soon. Our timing is off. Such is life. Don't worry about it. You didn't break my heart. That's for sure."

He gritted his teeth. There was nothing he could do. He messed up. Maybe tomorrow she'd stop being mad and continue to be his friend. He could only hope.

CHAPTER 19

"Oh my gosh, I can't believe you think that," Keleeja declared. "Daniel, she clearly didn't believe him."

He sucked up the last of his soda, shaking his head. "She did. He apologized, and he meant it. She understood where he was coming from."

"Did we even see the same movie? I'm starting to wonder if you fell asleep and dreamed an alternate ending."

He laughed. "Not with you sitting next to me."

"What's that supposed to mean?"

"Nothing."

She play-punched his arm, and he reached for her. She ducked out of reach, laughing.

"You're not getting away that easy."

He chased her. She tried to run, but his longer legs ate up the space between them. His strong arms encircled her, and he hauled her off her feet, swinging her around.

"Yikes! Don't do that. You're making me dizzy!" Not to mention the fact that being so close to his body was driving her body nuts.

She breathed his scent in deep, and her insides turned to mush. He smelled amazing, like aftershave and soap plus his natural scent. Her heart hammered out of control. Wow, was she lonely for a man's touch or what? One date and she was ready for more.

He set her gently on her feet. "Sorry. You okay?"

"I'm fine." She sounded breathless and tried to pull herself together.

"Would you like to grab dinner? I know it's kind of late but I could eat."

"Sure. Is there a good place open at this hour?"

He had picked her up earlier and they went straight to the movie. There wasn't much time for conversation then except a little bit in the car. So far, he'd been good, not mentioning his ex-wife.

"I know a place."

They ended up on the outskirts of downtown, in an area she wasn't familiar with. She looked around at a handful of darkened store windows. Above many of the closed shops were oversized windows that probably led to condos and such.

"Are you sure about this restaurant? Sometimes when I haven't been to an area for a few years, I go back to find they've torn down everything. This city is always changing."

"I'm sure. I was here a couple weeks ago. Wait until you taste the food."

"What kind of food?"

"Wait and see."

She wasn't picky when it came to food, although she knew what tasted good. Her curiosity increased when they turned down a street that looked more like an alley. At the least, there wouldn't be any parking.

A small unassuming shop came into view, tucked between two taller condo buildings. The name above the shop read *Roppongi*. A soft yellow glow illuminated the window, but she couldn't see into the place because of the material covering the store front windows.

"Japanese?" she asked as Daniel pulled the door open for her.

"Is that okay?"

"I love Japanese food. I don't get it often though."

"Good. I'm doing good so far." He winked at her.

She smirked.

The outside of the restaurant may have been plain and small, but the inside was another world. The narrow space stretched on longer than she would have thought. Against beautiful brick walls the manager had placed low round tables and plush cushions to sit on. There were no regular chairs in sight.

"If a person had trouble with their knees, they'd be in for it," she commented.

"Good thing we don't."

After they were seated, Daniel impressed her by asking for drinks in Japanese.

"Wow, are you fluent?"

He grinned. "Not really. I found the menu online and practiced that for two days. I thought about memorizing my food order, but you might ask me to order for you too."

She burst out laughing. "Then you'd have to memorize the entire menu."

"I should get points for my small effort."

"Whatever."

"Tough crowd."

She looked over the menu and found everything was written in Japanese. However, every offering included a photo. All one needed to do was point out a choice. Seemed like a good idea even for other restaurants, seeing ahead of time what the meal would look like.

"I feel like I'm in Tokyo," she said. "I love it. Why didn't I know about this place?"

"Few do, but like you said, everything is being redeveloped. I'm not sure how long this place will last. Let's take advantage of it while we can."

"Are you trying to say you'd like a second date?"

"Third… Forth…"

She liked him. He was friendly and easygoing. He smiled a lot and joked around. From the beginning, her sisters didn't run him off scared. He wanted a family and would accept hers. And yet, hesitation remained. There was no reason to assume this would go anywhere or think she'd want it to after a few dates. Better to take things slow.

Colin popped into her mind as he did several times even during the movie. She hadn't spoken to him for several days. He didn't text either, which made her wonder if their friendship had come to an end. When she last saw him, she was so mad, she felt like she never wanted to speak to him again. That feeling didn't last.

You're on a date, Keleeja. Stay in the moment.

"I'm going with this one." She pointed to a picture. "I think they're called gyoza or dumplings. I bought some from the grocery store a few times. They make them fresh. They're so juicy and salty and good."

"Potstickers," he agreed. "I like them too, but tonight I'm having chicken curry. The gyoza is more of an appetizer here. Do you want something else?"

They made their final choices, and soon Keleeja was filling her belly with delicious food. "Lord, if I eat like this every day, I'll be so fat."

His eyes twinkled. "You're beautiful either way."

"Thanks."

He flirted, and she found herself losing resistance to his charm. Conversation flowed as it did from the beginning with him. Something inside coiled, waiting for the shoe to drop, when he'd bring up his ex. It never came. His easy smile and beautiful blue eyes never wavered. He was perfect.

Could I fall for him?

Her heart did flutter, and her body responded. She wanted to let go and allow her emotions to follow. Daniel had changed just a little. From what she could see he seemed a little more available. Regardless she held back.

He leaned across the table and grasped her hand. Tingles raced down her spine. "What are you thinking? You're looking at me so intensely."

"You were talking. Shouldn't I pay attention?"

"I'm flattered. A man likes it when a woman hangs on his every word."

"You're in fantasyland now." She snickered because this sarcastic banter reminded her of how she joked around with Colin more than Daniel.

Why the heck am I thinking about Colin at a time like this?

"How about we go back to your place?" he suggested.

"What?"

"Sorry, I didn't mean that to sound like it did. I meant I'd like to see the girls."

"Too late. They're asleep."

He looked disappointed and then smiled. "Maybe at our next date."

"Oh were we going out again?"

"I'd like to think so. Am I wrong in assuming you're having a good time?"

"No, you're not wrong."

"Good. I'll drive you back to your car."

As they left the restaurant, she calmed down a little. Why not keep seeing him and let the relationship fall the way it would? She didn't have to decide to let herself care. His actions and words would dictate that. She could love him. Simple as that.

He took a minute to start the car, and she looked over at him, questioning whether she was wrong about the positive direction they were headed.

"Daniel? What's up?"

He reached across the space between them and brushed gentle fingers along her jaw. Another chill took her. What she gained in calm a minute ago flew out the window.

"You're so beautiful and perfect."

"Thanks, but I'm not perfect."

"Aren't you? I could go crazy over you."

Her heart stopped.

He removed his seatbelt. Her heart started up again and beat a wild tattoo. She swallowed hard. He closed the gap between them. Her gaze locked on his lips as he moved in. Her lips parted as she dragged in a tight breath. The air refused to fill her lungs, although his delicious scent filled her nostrils.

With millimeters between their mouths, she turned her head. The kiss landed on her cheek. He gasped and drew back. She stared hard out the window.

He uttered a nervous laugh. "Did I misread the atmosphere between us?"

"No, um…" She couldn't think of an excuse. In fact, she didn't know why she turned away. Her body was telling her to go for it. A kiss wasn't that big a deal. She'd done a lot more than that in her dating history. So what was up with her? "I'm sorry. I should get back home. I still have a little way to go after we get to my car."

"I said I would pick you up. You refused." He sounded annoyed. She didn't blame him. Probably confused. Well, he could join the club.

They returned to her car, and she jumped in with a brief "goodnight" and headed home.

"Guess I won't see him again. Dang, we were going so well. Why would I act like a shy little virgin at one kiss? What's the big deal? I mean, do you want to find someone or not, Keleeja?"

Her cell phone dinged, and at a stop light, she checked the screen. The text was from Daniel.

"Can we try again Friday night?"

She grinned.

Colin's office door opened, and his best friend strolled in. "Hey, you ready?"

"Just a sec." Colin started to close out the screen on his computer and then hesitated. He'd located five of the girls he dated in the past. All he needed to do was shoot off a DM. The indecision drove him crazy. "Do you remember Janice?"

Daniel parked on the edge of his desk. "The girl with the nose?"

Colin frowned. "There was nothing wrong with her nose."

"She looked like she used to be a kickboxing champion and got kicked in it one too many times."

"I thought you were the nice one between the two of us."

His friend shrugged and then laughed. "I've got my moments. So what about her?"

"I was thinking of contacting her. I need a date for

dad's sixtieth birthday party. And you never said if you were going. Are you?"

"Of course. Your dad is a great guy. I like him. I'll be there."

"Are you bringing…"

Daniel watched his face, curiosity in his eyes. "If she'll say yes. I'll bring Keleeja."

Colin busied himself closing his laptop. He and Daniel were going for a drink and maybe shoot some pool afterward. They hadn't hung out for a while since Colin filled up his time with work, and Daniel was busy dating Keleeja.

Why did the fact that they were a couple bug him so much? Maybe because he missed his chance. He was the one who backed off. No, he ran, and it irked him. He wasn't the type to run from a woman. At the same time, he admitted the timing wasn't right for the two of them. Regardless, over the last three months, she never left his mind.

He remembered every smile, every laugh, every detail of their conversations. At least he could have kept their friendship up, but he felt guilty for letting her down. She deserved better than him. She deserved Daniel, so he tried not to sweat it. And Daniel seemed to be good and truly over Isabella.

"You said you were okay with us dating," Daniel said.

"What?" Colin pretended to check inside his desk for something. "Of course. I didn't say anything, did I?"

"No, but… I don't know. Sometimes I get the feeling you don't like me seeing her. You'd say something if you were against it, right? We haven't gotten in each other's way since high school."

Colin stood and smacked his friend on the shoulder. "Don't sweat it, man. If anybody's rooting for you to find the right girl, it's me. But you'll have to really turn on the charm to get her to have eight kids for you though."

Daniel snorted. "I'm not hoping for eight kids."

"Nine?"

"Ten."

They both laughed.

Colin managed to dismiss the conflicting thoughts. This was Daniel, his best friend, and he wanted him to find happiness. Colin had lots of time to get over Sherrie and maybe think about finding someone new in the future. In fact, there were times he felt normal and even happy. Four months had brought him a long way, and he couldn't even identify with that guy in the parking lot when Keleeja rescued him.

Stop. You're doing it again, thinking about her.

He spent the evening with Daniel, but when it came time to go home to his empty house, he chose not to go. Instead, he returned to his office to run a couple background checks for clients. At midnight, his phone rang.

"Isabella? Of all the... What does she want?" He started to ignore the call but changed his mind. Better to see where her head was. "What do you want?"

"Hi, Colin. It's been a while." The sweet tone made him grind his teeth.

"Get to the point."

"I was sorry to hear about your fiancée. She was a nice person, perfect for you."

"Isabella!"

She coughed. "I wanted to ask you about Daniel."

"No."

"You don't know what I was going to say."

"You're obsessed with him for some reason, even though you've had other men—we both know that's true, that there's been more than one. Why don't you let him go and be with someone else? Your heart is as black as the midnight sky, but try to put him before yourself."

"If you're done insulting me…"

"I can go on all night."

"I don't have to take this from you!"

"No, you don't. Goodbye."

"Colin, wait. *Please.*"

Despite his better judgement, he didn't hang up.

"I want to talk to Daniel. I know, I know. You want me to leave him alone, but I just need a minute of his time. He's been seeing someone else, hasn't he? I saw them downtown one day, coming out of that Japanese restaurant we used to like."

He tensed. Daniel took Keleeja to the restaurant he used to frequent with his ex-wife? Then again, why not? He shouldn't have to give up good food because the witch used to go there with him.

"She's a Black woman," Isabella went on.

"How is that any of your business?"

"I never thought he would go that way. It's surprising, that's all. But maybe he's experimenting. I've done a lot of that myself in the past."

"You've got three seconds."

She rushed on. "Your dad is having a birthday party on Saturday, isn't he?"

He froze. "You're not invited. Don't try to cling to him using my family, Isabella. You'll regret it."

"Your family has always welcomed me as your best friend's wife."

"That's over."

"I felt like they could almost be my family." She laughed.

This woman wasn't hearing him. She had a one-tracked mind. All her thoughts were about herself and what she wanted. It gagged him to the point of being unable to speak.

"Listen to me closely, Isabella." He bit out the words one at a time. "Don't-come. Don't-call. Stay-away-from-Daniel. *Forever.* Goodbye."

He disconnected and started to call Daniel until he remembered the lateness of the hour. Daniel had said he had a five a.m. pickup to drive a client to the airport. He'd have to get up even earlier than that. Colin let him sleep. They could discuss his crazy ex-wife another time.

CHAPTER 21

Colin's family. Butterflies stirred in Keleeja's belly. She hadn't eaten anything all day, knowing Daniel was taking her to Colin's father's birthday party. It wasn't even like this was Daniel's family. So why was she so nervous? She didn't have to impress them or for them to like her. Tell that to her nerves. They were a mess.

"What's the big deal anyway?"

She thought about Colin. Both annoyance and sadness rose inside. She missed chatting with him and his smile, the way his eyes twinkled when he was amused. He wasn't amused often back when they were talking, but there were times. She wondered if he smiled more now that time had passed. She hoped so.

"Stop, Keleeja. Why in the world are you thinking about him anyway?"

Daniel was sweet to her. He was thoughtful, and he took her to dinner at least once a week. She refused to tax Autumn's niceness with asking her to babysit too much, but she and Daniel spoke on the phone too.

Keleeja avoided bringing Daniel over to the house. She wanted to wait until she knew their relationship was going somewhere. It was probably silly since the girls already met him, but regardless. They didn't need to get more attached to him until she was sure he wouldn't disappear.

She checked herself out in the mirror. This afternoon, she wore jeans and a simple blouse. Casual. That's what Daniel had said about the party. No one would dress up because the family and friends were all getting together at Colin's parents' house. It was Colin's dad's sixtieth birthday, and his wife was throwing him a surprise party.

"Ugh. Why am I going? I should just stay home."

No, she wasn't a coward, and truth was, she wanted to see Colin, to know he was doing fine. She hadn't spoken to him in three months.

"He might even have a new girlfriend."

That thought threw her. She stood there for a minute, not moving, trying to assess what she thought about Colin having a new woman in his life. Her mind refused to examine it, so she continued to get ready for the party.

The doorbell rang. That would be Daniel, arriving too early. If nothing else, tonight would be memorable.

"KELEEJA, NICE TO MEET YOU. COME IN, COME IN."

Keleeja tried not to gape at Colin's mom, but she felt her eyes widening as she stepped into the house. The woman was a female version of Colin—tall and beautiful. Same smile, same silver eyes reflected Colin in vivid detail. "Hello, nice to meet you, Mrs. Voss."

She chuckled and waved a hand. "Oh, don't be so formal. Call me Minerva."

"Um, Minerva. Thanks for having me." Keleeja held up the small, gift-wrapped box she held. "This is for Mr. Voss. I wasn't sure what to get, but I didn't want to come empty-handed."

"You didn't have to do that but thank you so much. I'm sure whatever it is, Bernard will love it. Daniel, give me a hug. I should be mad at you for not stopping by often enough."

Daniel hugged her, grinning. "Sorry, Mom. You're always on my mind."

She drew back and chattered away as she led them down the hall. Behind her back, Keleeja raised her eyebrows at Daniel and mouthed "Mom?"

He shrugged and whispered. "She's been like a mom to me since the day I met her. I enjoy calling her that because she likes it."

"I don't blame you." Keleeja always felt a little sad meeting mothers who were involved in their kids' lives and cared about them. She wondered how she survived growing up with a mother like hers, who was more interested in herself than anyone else.

"Daniel, you go on ahead for a minute," Minerva told him. "I want to chat with Keleeja."

Just before reaching a room with several voices

emanating, Minerva hooked her arm with Keleeja's and held her back. Daniel winked at Keleeja and headed into the room. A cheer rose, several people calling out his name. Apparently, the man was popular and well-known among Colin's family and friends.

"Keleeja, I wanted to thank you."

She gasped and focused on Minerva. "What for?"

"No, don't minimize it." A frown marred her brow, and tears filled her eyes. "If it wasn't for you, I might have lost my sweet Colin."

Keleeja realized what she meant and flushed. "I only reached out like any decent person would, Minerva. You don't have to thank me."

"I do! Both Bernard and I are extremely grateful you were there that day. Colin told us everything. When I forced him to come to the family dinner, he told us about the day he spent at your place. He even told us about you teaching him to fold laundry."

She laughed, and Keleeja joined her.

"Do you know how many of his teenage years I tried to get that boy to fold his own clothes? And failed, I might add. Now that I think about it, you accomplished two miracles that day."

Keleeja snorted. "Wow, I didn't realize it was such a thing."

"Don't get me started. But seriously, thank you. Colin has always been like his father, very strong, very independent. He doesn't like leaning on others. He works through everything on his own, mastering his emotions. Then after the fact, he comes to us like nothing's amiss. That's not what family is for."

"I agree. Family is for love and support, especially during the rough times."

"Exactly. We see eye-to-eye on that! I can see you're a good girl, someone we can welcome into the family. Daniel is very lucky to have found you."

Relief washed over Keleeja—and regret. She had wondered how Colin's family would respond to her, being Black. Although she was seeing Daniel and not their son, she'd heard Daniel was close to the family. They were bound to have opinions and views on the relationship. Minerva's words reassured her.

"Now, we better get in there. They might sneak into the food before my husband gets home. I have to keep my eye on them, especially my boys."

Her words registered on Keleeja's brain. She referred to her sons, including Colin, and then Keleeja saw him. An odd wave of something shook her, but she quickly schooled her features into a friendly smile and greeted everyone.

Colin stood near the fireplace with another man an inch or so shorter. They appeared to be twins for a second, and then Keleeja saw the differences. The other guy was probably a little older. Colin's shoulders were broader, jaw firmer, eyes clearer, and he exuded much more confidence.

She caught her breath and shifted her gaze away from him after a brief smile and nod of acknowledgement. Attraction—that was the feeling, and she had missed him. The emotion was stronger than it needed to be, but Colin was so fun to talk to and to tease. He was honest and open, yet forceful and headstrong too.

He was ignorant of simple things and knowledgeable about a lot more. She could learn from him and teach him at the same time.

"Keleeja?"

"Huh?" She snapped to attention when Daniel spoke to her. "Sorry, what?"

He studied her face. "I said, this is Colin's sister and two brothers."

Keleeja listened as intently as she could to the introductions, trying to remember the names of Colin's siblings and their spouses. Colin was the only unmarried one of the four, but he was the second born.

After the deluge of meeting so many, Colin made his way over to her. "Hey."

"Hey," she breathed.

He hugged her, and she settled for just a second against his chest. Out of the corner of her eye, she met Minerva's gaze and thought she saw recognition there. Keleeja pulled back quickly.

"Been awhile, Colin. Are you doing okay?"

"I'm great. Thanks."

They were so weird and awkward. She willed herself to stop it and be natural. At this rate, anyone watching their interaction would think she was fooling around with Colin behind Daniel's back. Not that she and Daniel were all that serious yet. Still, she didn't want any misunderstandings.

"He's coming," someone shouted.

The chatter in the room rose, and Minerva shushed them all. "Quiet, everyone. Remember when he comes in, you shout 'Surprise!'"

"We know, Mom." The brother who looked so much like Colin smirked. "That's a given."

She glared at him, and everyone laughed.

A few moments later, Keleeja heard the front door open and close, then footsteps in the hall. She wondered if Colin got any of his features from his dad. Was the older man as nice as his wife? Her mind wandered over the possibilities, and then he appeared.

"Surprise!"

"I knew you were up to something, Minerva." He laughed, and the deep rumbling sound was exactly like Colin's, just a little scratchier with age. "This is a nice surprise, and look who I found outside. Come on. You aren't the shy type. Come say hello."

No one needed to tell Keleeja who it was. An ethereal beauty with dark hair and big pretty eyes, although her cheeks were fuller than Keleeja had imagined. She had dressed up in a form-fitting outfit and high heels, standing out against everyone else in casual wear.

Minerva's expression darkened, and she pressed her lips into a thin line. At Keleeja's side, Daniel stiffened. She felt the tension rolling off him.

She curled a hand over her mouth, pretending to cover a cough. "Who's that?" she asked to confirm her suspicions.

He forced his response from a clenched jaw. "Isabella."

olin's smile vanished, and he thrust his way through the crowd of his family and friends. "What are you doing here, Isabella? I thought I told you—"

"This is for you, Mr. Bernard." Isabella totally ignored Colin as she handed his father a gift bag with red tissue paper sticking up from the top. From the looks of it she'd stuffed the bag full with his present. "Happy birthday, sir. You don't look a day over fifty-nine."

Someone in the crowd chuckled.

Colin reached for her arm to whip her around to face him. "I said what are you doing here?"

"Whoa, whoa, Colin." Daniel stepped forward. "Calm down, man. You don't need to manhandle her. I'm sure she's just trying to support—"

"You're still defending her after all she's put you through? Maybe you forgot you came here with Keleeja."

Daniel flushed. "Of course I didn't. I'm just saying calm down. We don't need to focus on this at your dad's party."

Keleeja tried to decide if she agreed with Colin's assessment of Daniel's actions. Daniel was a super nice person. He was sweet almost to a fault. He wouldn't like even his enemies to be hurt. That was her conclusion about his personality over the last three months. So if she looked at this situation logically, why wouldn't he stop Colin from being too rough and angry with Isabella?

At the same time, I can't help feeling like he's back to it again, preferring her.

Keleeja clamped her teeth together and concentrated on not showing her jealousy and frustration. One minute she felt comfortable with Daniel and happy about where they were headed. But the second she started feeling that way, something happened to tip her off balance.

"I need to talk to you, Daniel." Isabella's tone exuded sweet innocence.

Keleeja would have to be deaf, dumb, and blind to believe the persona Isabella projected. She didn't even know Isabella to figure out this woman breathed manipulation.

"It's important," Isabella insisted.

Colin swore under his breath. "And you chose my dad's birthday party to tell him. You have his number. You could have called him, arranged a meeting. No, you have to be the center of attention, and what better place other than a party?"

Colin's siblings started speaking up, agreeing with his statement that their father's party wasn't the place.

"Now, now." Minerva clapped her hands to get everyone's attention. "We don't want to turn Bernard's happy day into a fiasco. Let's get back to the celebration, and Daniel can decide for himself what he wants to do. Bernard, dear, come in. Look at all the presents everyone brought you. And wait until you taste the cake. It's your favorite!"

Bernard's eyes glowed. "Strawberries and cream?"

"What else?" His wife winked at him.

Keleeja liked the two of them even more. Maybe it was because she never failed to make her girls' favorite cake on their birthdays, and it was always a big production.

Daniel drew her attention from the older couple back to the drama. "I don't have anything to say to you, Isabella. Just go. This isn't the time or place."

"You wouldn't answer my calls or my texts," Isabella told him.

"With good reason." He touched Keleeja's lower back. "I've moved on. We're not even married anymore —by your doing. Let it go."

He started to turn away, prompting Keleeja to do the same.

"I'm pregnant."

The entire room went silent.

Keleeja's head spun. Blood rushed through her ears, making it impossible to hear. She questioned whether her mind played tricks on her and stared at Isabella then Daniel. He'd gone pale, eyes wide, mouth open.

After a moment, Keleeja's hearing kicked back in. Isabella dug through her purse and pulled out a rumpled sheet of paper. "I have the test to prove it and my doctor's office number. I've given them permission to share my medical results with you. You can call them and verify that I'm telling the truth. I'm pregnant, Daniel. I'm having your baby."

"Let's go. *Now!*" Colin grabbed hold of Keleeja and Daniel and charged them toward the door. "You come too, Isabella!"

In seconds, Keleeja found herself in a smaller room with the door shut against the partygoers. The four of them stood in the middle of a cozy living room. The basket of various colored yarns on the floor by an armchair said Minerva made use of the room often. Perhaps Bernard joined her to watch TV in the evenings.

Keleeja realized she avoided reality when she focused on their surroundings and forced her attention back to Daniel possibly being a father. Isabella clung to his arm, tears on the ends of her fake lashes.

"I didn't mean for this to happen. I wasn't ready. I said I was, but you know… And it's happened. I was as shocked as you." She sniffed. "Say something, Daniel."

He found his voice at last. "How do you know it's mine?"

"Because I'm three months pregnant, and there hasn't been anyone else for six months! You know Evan left me."

Keleeja found a chair and sank into it. Colin moved next to her and touched her arm. "Are you okay?"

She dropped her face into her hand. "I shouldn't be here. This is none of my business."

"It *is* your business. You've been dating him, and you should know what she's up to. If it means anything, I don't believe her. She'd sink to these levels to keep a hold on him. But I thought she'd let him go when we didn't hear from her all this time."

Keleeja had a small glimmer of hope when she thought Isabella could be lying, but it died a quick death. What was the point? Either the woman was telling the truth, and Daniel would have a connection to her forever, or she was lying which meant she was crazy and would force a connection forever. Either way, Keleeja didn't want the drama. Besides, manipulation using pregnancy left a bitter taste in her mouth leftover from her own mother. She couldn't tolerate even the thought of it.

When she didn't hear anything for a few moments, Keleeja looked up. Daniel stood frozen in front of Isabella. His gaze flitted between her face, searching it for the lie and then down to her belly in wonder. Keleeja didn't have to read his mind to know what he was thinking. He wanted it to be true. He wanted a family more than anything. She got the message real fast that it didn't have to be with her. She was done.

"I need to go," she whispered and struggled to her feet. Colin moved to help her, but she drew away. Her mood was so low she didn't want to be touched or talk to anyone. It irked her to feel like this when she had just met Colin's family and wanted to get to know them. She didn't want to bring anyone else down with her attitude.

"He'll take you," Colin ground out. "Won't you, Daniel?"

"Huh?" He gazed at them with a blank expression then blinked. Recognition lit his eyes. "Keleeja, you have to understand. I need to be sure. I have to talk to her."

So forget me? Is that it?

She sighed. "I get it. Goodnight, Daniel."

"You can't take a minute to drive her home? You brought her here!"

Keleeja laid a hand on Colin's arm. "It's fine, Colin. I can take a taxi. Just go back to your dad's party. I'm good. I've been taking care of myself all this time. And it's not like I'm stranded in the middle of nowhere."

A muscle jumped in Colin's jaw, and he clenched his hands into fists. He was getting way more worked up than he needed to. Keleeja admitted if only to herself that Daniel's response to taking her home hurt. She agreed with Colin. He could take a minute to run her home. He could reassure her that even if Isabella was pregnant, that wouldn't affect the two of them. Instead, he couldn't even think straight.

Maybe she should cut him some slack and be patient. He had a shock—a good one. Instead, she wanted to throw up and fuss at him as much as Colin was doing. She wanted to tell Isabella what a low-down piece of garbage she thought she was. It didn't matter.

She made her excuses to Colin's parents and managed to extract herself from the partyers as quickly as possible. In the driveway, she pulled her phone out to call a taxi. A big hand covered hers to stop her, and she looked up expecting Colin. Daniel stood at her side.

"I'll take you home."

He didn't speak as he drove. Tension in the car set her teeth on edge, and the back of her head ached. She recognized the pain as stress.

"Daniel—"

"Don't." He pushed a hand through his hair. "I'm sorry, Keleeja. I'm not ready to talk. I'm in shock, and I don't know what to think."

"Of course." Bile rose in her throat, along with resentment against him. She tried to be a bigger woman and failed.

At her house, he pulled into the drive but didn't put the car in park. He kept the engine running and said nothing. A string of insults ran through her mind, but she got out of the car. The very second she slammed the door, he peeled out of the drive and was gone.

"So eager to get back to her. Ugh, what am I doing?"

When she let herself in the house, Lola catapulted into her arms. Keleeja staggered a little.

"Goodness, girl. You're getting big."

"Can I have a piece of cake, Lee?"

"You had cake earlier with lunch. You said you didn't want to wait until dinner. You're not getting cake all day long."

Her lower lip poked out, and Keleeja's phone dinged. She set the little girl on her feet. The text came from Colin.

"I'm calling you after things settle down here. Answer."

"Wow, bossy much?" And then she laughed, thinking about how she had spoken to him when he was in trouble. She wasn't feeling that low, but it amused her that he would use her technique. "I guess turnabout is fair play."

After she made up an excuse to Autumn for being home so early, she went to her room. In a little bit, she'd thank Autumn and send her home then get the girls settled in bed. Right then, she wasn't feeling anything but sorry for herself.

She laid on the bed and buried her face in a pillow. The frustrated scream didn't come. Instead, she cried just a tiny bit. Not because she loved Daniel. She wasn't there yet. Her feelings were bruised, and it felt like nothing would ever work out in the relationship department. She was seeing a future where the girls would grow up and live their own lives, and she would be stuck alone and lonely.

"I'm being melodramatic now."

She yawned and dozed off.

The next thing she knew, she was waking up. She didn't know how much time had passed. Her phone rang, flashing Colin's name. Crud. She forgot to let Autumn know she was free to go. While answering the call, she shouted down the stairs.

"Hey, Autumn. I'm sorry. You can get going. I've got them."

No answer. The TV was turned down low, and the house lay in stillness. She checked the time on her phone. Shoot, the girls must be asleep, and she might have awakened them with her big mouth.

"Keleeja, are you there? Hello?"

"Oh sorry, Colin," she whispered. "I have no idea what's going on. I fell asleep. Let me check on the girls and Autumn real quick and call you back."

He hesitated. "Is that an excuse? If you don't call, I'm showing up at your door."

She laughed. "Thanks. But that's not necessary. I want to talk to you. I've kind of missed my friend."

"Yeah." He cleared his throat. "Me too."

CHAPTER 23

"You were so angry with Daniel."

Colin leaned against the kitchen island, taking a break after bringing in all the dishes from the dining room. His mom rinsed dishes at the sink and put them in the dishwasher.

"I've never seen you that way with your best friend." Her brow wrinkled in concentration. "No, there was that one time back in high school. If I'm not mistaken, that was over a girl too."

"Too?" He grumbled under his breath. "Mom, you must admit he was being a jerk to Keleeja. And none of you like Isabella. You yourself pegged her as a manipulative—"

"*Colin.*"

"—from the beginning."

"True, but we're talking about you."

He sighed.

She paused and rested a hand on her hip while wagging a glove-covered finger at him. "I know my children. I know *you*, Colin. There's more to it than you're letting on."

"I don't know what you're talking about."

"I saw it in the way she responded to you as well."

He stilled. Something inside stirred, but he tamped it down. Sure, he liked Keleeja—a lot. She was a great friend, and he would be lying if he didn't admit that he found her very attractive. But it hadn't been but a few months since he lost Sherrie. He was *not* looking for someone new.

"She's a friend, Mom. I'm not fighting Daniel for her."

"I liked Keleeja from the start. The way she speaks and the way she behaves, she seems like an intelligent and kind person. Of course, she won my heart the minute I learned she helped you in your most difficult time. It should have been us, but you were always a stubborn one. Even when you were born, you showed your stubbornness, coming two weeks early."

He braced for a long story he heard a thousand times.

"I'm not getting into that. You don't have to look so pained!"

He chuckled.

"You defended her against Daniel."

"He was wrong. He should have reassured her and thrown that witch out of the house. You raised us to be gentleman, didn't you?"

She snorted. "You talk about being a gentleman while suggesting manhandling a woman."

"You know what I mean."

"Yes, I do. Anyway, don't try to fool your mother. I've been here a lot longer. Keleeja is special. I can see it. But you've never been a man who went after another man's partner."

"I'm not."

"Good."

He felt like he couldn't win in this conversation. In fact, he'd never won an argument with his mom.

"That aside," she continued. "Daniel is in a tough place. If Isabella is pregnant, he has to keep her in his life. Not as his wife, but there is that connection. And it'll put stress on the relationship with Keleeja. Daniel is sweet, but he's also an innocent in many ways. He can't see his world beyond that silly Isabella. You'd think he would see it by now at his age. Maybe he would if she gave him two seconds to collect himself."

"I agree."

"Now a child complicates things."

"She's got to be lying!"

"She wasn't lying. I've seen her lying many times, and that light in her eyes… No, she's pregnant. To think an innocent child having a mom like her."

"Keleeja's mom is similar."

Her eyebrows rose. "Is she? Tell me about her. Not the mom but Keleeja."

He spent some time sharing about Keleeja's home life and about his time with her and the kids. Being so close with his family, he had always freely shared information about his life. At first, he tried to hold back regarding Keleeja. If there was something special he felt about her, he didn't want his family finding out. As his mom prodded him, he opened up.

"Well, we're done here, Colin. Thanks for helping me. You can go hang out with your dad if you like."

"He said he was exhausted and would lay down."

She smiled. "I bet he is. He thrives on all the attention from his family."

Colin said goodnight and left his parents' house to head home. Keleeja came to mind again, and he remembered his mom's warning to leave her alone. That wasn't happening. He worried about Daniel's reaction to learning he would be a dad. If Isabella wasn't lying, Daniel would be in a tough spot when it came to Keleeja. And she, he could only imagine what must be going through her head.

Once he'd showered and laid across his bed, he phoned her. He wondered if she would ignore his call, but she answered right away. Her shout surprised him.

"Keleeja, are you there? Hello?"

"Oh sorry, Colin. I have no idea what's going on."

The sultry quality of her voice stirred his attraction to her, but she said she fell asleep. She wasn't coming on to him, unfortunately. He chuckled under his breath at the idea.

Soon they settled into conversation the way they did before losing contact. She was easy to talk to and joke around with. He could forget about the past and even work issues. Keleeja kept his attention with the way she spoke, her ideas and thoughts about life and people.

"I can't believe the triplets are going into kinder-garten in a few months. They're growing up."

"Kids do that. My nieces and nephews grew a foot over one summer."

"That's how it goes. Wait, didn't you say one of your nieces is about the triplets' age? Maybe we can get them together to play sometime."

"Sure. I don't usually take any of them off my sister-in-law's hands, but she'll probably agree."

"Colin, you should be a better uncle!"

"I'm their favorite. I buy the best gifts."

"You're not serious, are you?"

"I'm very serious."

"Lord, I have so much to teach you."

He grinned. "I look forward to it."

He realized the innocent words could be taken another way. That was the way it was with them, and any male-female friendship. Could he be just friends with her and nothing more, especially with her seeing Daniel?

"Oh!"

He worried he offended her. "What is it?"

"Nothing. It's Daniel calling."

"If you have to go…"

She hesitated. "No."

"Keleeja."

"*No.*" She spoke more firmly. "I need a minute from him. I get that he was shocked and needed to process what Isabella told him. But I'm human too. I'm mad. I'm hurt. You name it."

"Of course you are. Do you want to talk about it?"

Women usually wanted to talk things out. He tended to clam up until he got a hold of his emotions.

"Will it get on your nerves if I vent a little?"

"No. Go ahead. You were there for me. The least I can do is return the favor."

"But I hate when people obsess over their exes with someone new."

"Is he an ex?"

"We're in limbo. Probably. I don't know."

"And I'm not someone new. I'm a friend." Putting himself in the friend zone didn't sit right.

"You're more than a friend to me, Colin. I'm sorry we stopped talking. I'm not trying to imply I'm jumping from Daniel to you. That's not what I mean."

"I know. Don't overthink it. Talk. It's fine."

She laughed. "Yes, sir!"

The hours passed. The night grew later. Still they talked. He didn't want to get off the phone, even when his eyelids drooped, and he kept losing track of the conversation. She too fell silent, and her breathing indicated sleep. She'd pop awake and continue chatting, denying a wish to go to bed.

The next thing he knew daylight streamed through the window, and he checked his phone. It was dead. He grinned.

Keleeja.

"I can't believe this! Not now." Tears filled Keleeja's eyes, and she blinked a few times to clear them away. This also wasn't the time to fall apart.

The stranger tapped on her window, and she groaned before climbing out of the car.

"Are you okay, ma'am?"

"I'm fine," she bit out. "But I'm in a hurry. I can't believe you hit me!"

"I'm sorry. You look fine though."

She glared at him while stomping to the back of her car, where this man rear-ended her. Still grumbling under her breath, she pulled her phone out and dialed Autumn. No answer. That's right. She was in a meeting with the president and VP of her company. It would take a miracle for her to get out of the meetings to make the performance tonight.

What am I going to do?

The entire back seat of her car was full of bags.

She'd been assigned to pick up several last-minute items the school needed for the program her sisters were performing in that night. These people needed to be more organized. And it wasn't like she was some housewife whose entire existence revolved around the children's schedules.

"Listen, sir, no harm done, right? Why don't we just forget this happened. I can get on my way, and you can get on yours."

The older gentleman's eyes widened. "Oh, no. We can't do that. We must get a police report. This is a company car. Do you know how much trouble I would be in if I don't handle this properly? I need this job."

"And I need my girls' program to go off without a hitch. I said I could handle the last-minute shopping. I'm *not* going to disappoint them. Not to mention the fact that I have to get over there and pick them up and take them home to change. Ugh, so much in one day…"

Stress pain started at the base of her neck and worked its way up. She rubbed the spot. The man was already shaking his head no and cutting her off. He didn't care one bit about her problems.

"Sir—"

He held up a hand, pressing his phone to his ear. "Yes, I want to report an accident…"

Keleeja groaned.

What about Colin? Could he? *Would* he help? He made his own schedule, but even so his work kept him busy. She'd never asked him for help, although they had been close friends for a while now. She didn't push for him to get closer to the girls. Still he played Uno or some other game with them every time he came to the house. Nervy little Lola insisted on that.

Would it bother him if she asked?

Her cell phone rang, and she gasped. Colin seemed to sense her need.

"Um, hey, Colin."

"How about Chinese tonight? I bought a new game I think the girls will like."

"Tonight?" Oh yeah, she didn't tell him about the program.

"Sorry. You're probably busy. I didn't mean to be inconsiderate. Once an idea pops into my head, I go after it." He chuckled.

"Colin, I've had a little bit of a fender-bender and—"

"Are you okay?" She heard the sheer terror in his voice and could have chewed her tongue off. Too late, she recalled he lost his fiancée to a car accident.

"Yes, I'm great. No injuries at all. It wasn't that serious. But the other driver is insisting we wait for the police to do a report, and I need help. I wouldn't ask."

"I'm on my way. Say where."

"Wait, Colin. Calm down."

"*Where, Keleeja.*"

The desperation and panic didn't ease. She wouldn't calm him down until he set eyes on her. The best she could do was let him come to where she was and reassure himself. Her schedule was shot, and she had to accept that.

"Alright." She gave him directions, and twenty minutes later, he was dragging her into his arms. Her protest fell on deaf ears. "Colin, I can't breathe."

He drew back, cupped her face, and stared down into her eyes. A tingle of pleasure washed over her. To see such concern for her stole her reason.

"See?" She smiled at him. "I'm okay. Still here waiting for the police after an eternity, but fine nonetheless."

He nodded agreement, and tension seemed to ease out of him. He checked the damage to the car, or lack thereof and had a brief conversation with the other driver. She leaned against the side of her car, which rocked gently every time another car zoomed past. Everyone was getting to their destinations just fine, and she was stuck.

"I'm afraid he won't see reason," Colin told her. "I can wait with you. The police will be here soon."

"No, Colin. Please. I don't want to ask this, but I was wondering if you wouldn't mind picking up the girls and taking them home. They have a program tonight, and they've got to get ready. Plus, I have this stuff the school needs and—"

To her horror, she sniffed, and the tears fell. He dragged her against his chest again and held her tight.

"I'll do whatever you want."

She struggled against the emotions threatening to take control because of his words.

It's just the stress, Keleeja. Stop right there.

"Don't cry," he whispered. "I'll get them, and I'll take the supplies to the school."

She pulled herself together. "I would never ask, but Autumn is in meetings all day. Ever since she took over her boss' job, it's been nonstop. I'm happy for her."

"But you never get a break anymore?"

"The girls are my responsibility. Autumn's help was a blessing."

"You've got me." He grinned and then frowned. "Why didn't you tell me about the school thing?"

"I didn't think you'd be interested."

Disappointment flashed in his expression. "I don't look like the reliable type when it comes to kids?"

"It's not that."

He opened the rear door of her car and began unloading everything. "You'll need to call the school and let them know I'm coming. Hopefully, there won't be too much fuss since I'm not one of the people listed for picking them up."

"I'll clear everything."

She was sorry for insulting him, but it was important to her not to assume or to take advantage of him. Leaning on someone else was too easy, especially when the girls drove her nuts. They were a huge responsibility and not Colin's. He and she were friends, and she loved spending time with him. If she put too much on him and ran him off, it would kill her.

He listened to some last-minute instructions and kissed her cheek then he was off. A minute after he was gone, the police finally showed up. She suffered through explaining what happened, signed something, and after another eon, was able to get back on the road.

Colin texted her to say he was at home with the girls, so she headed there rather than to the school. A short while later she burst through the front door.

Jackets, bookbags, and shoes were strewn everywhere. The remnants of a candy wrapper lay on the floor, and Keleeja snatched it up frowning.

She hurried to the second floor where all the chatter came from and found that another hurricane had hit the girls' bedroom. Colin knelt in the middle of the rug, pulling the felt tree costume over Lily's head. One of Lily's arms extended in the air, and the other seemed to be pinned to her side. Her muffled voice came from inside as she tried to give Colin directions.

Lola scrambled under the bed, looking for something. Tawney curled beneath her bedsheets, reading a book. Lara's whining came from the bathroom.

Keleeja bit back a laugh. "What in the world is going on here? Have you girls lost your mind?"

"Lee," Lily wailed. "I can't get my costume on."

Colin looked up and grinned. "Welcome home. I promise I was going to clean up as soon as I finished helping her."

Keleeja shook her head. "First of all, she doesn't need to put that on until later in the program. They first need to be dressed in white shirts and dark skirts for the concert."

"Oh." He looked disappointed. "I liked the leaves on the branches."

She snorted. "I'm not fooled. Ever since I finished making that costume, Lily's been desperate to get into it. She convinced you she needed to wear it to school. Thanks so much for your help, but I'm here now. Why don't you head downstairs and grab a piece of cake or something. I'll be down in a minute."

"Can I keep helping?"

She looked at him in surprise. "Really?"

"Yeah." He rubbed the back of his neck. "If it's okay, I mean. I'm not a weirdo or anything."

"Dummy." She laughed. "I know you're not. We've talked enough and hung out here so often, I know better. Alright, if you're not just being polite…"

"I'm not."

"Great. Let's get back on schedule."

"Aye aye, Captain." He saluted.

Lola came out from under the bed to jump onto his back. "Aye aye, Captain."

"Lola!"

"I can't find my shoes, Lee. Can I go barefoot?"

"No."

"Can I wear my costume since Lily's wearing hers?"

"*No.*"

She whined.

"No whining, all of you." Keleeja sighed. "See, Colin. Before the night is over, you'll wish you weren't so nice."

Keleeja sat at Colin's side and peeked at him every so often. He stared at the kids performing on the stage, a big grin on his face and wonder in his eyes. One would think he'd never been to a children's program. Maybe he never appreciated it so much.

The young voices rung out in song, so pure and sweet. Her heart ached to watch her sisters. Lola, the ham, threw her arms up with extra gusto and stamped a foot forward when all the others moved uncertainly. That girl would drive her batty when she was a teenager.

Colin touched her hand and drew her attention. A chill raced down her spine. He leaned closer, and his aftershave tickled her nostrils. "Look at Lola," he whispered. "She loves being the center of attention."

"Don't I know it."

He chuckled under his breath, shaking his head. "And Lara. She's just mouthing the words."

"Bet she forgot some of them, and she's a little nervous with everybody looking. I'm surprised she got up there."

"I coached her."

She blinked at him. "You? When?"

"Just before we left the house. I told her she's beautiful and talented and can do everything Lola does."

Keleeja's mouth fell open. "I don't remember that."

"It was when you went back for Tawney's bag."

"Wow, thanks so much. You've been a big help."

"Quiet!" One of the parents in their row shushed them, and Keleeja decided to keep her expression of gratitude until later. Just saying thanks wasn't enough for what Colin's friendship had meant to her over the months.

He took her hand and squeezed it gently before hanging onto it. She wondered at the touch, trying not to take it wrong. All this time, she kept rehearsing in her head that they were nothing more than friends. She wouldn't entertain the idea that they could be more.

She refused to disappoint herself. Not when it hadn't been a year since he lost his fiancée, and after that fiasco with Daniel. She was the one who pushed Daniel away because she couldn't handle him and Isabella and their child. He tried to talk to her a few times, but she wouldn't bite. Better to be alone, she'd thought.

She didn't put too much pressure on her friendship with Colin either. Regardless, here he was at her girls' program.

Friendship, friendship, friendship. We're friends!

The mantra refused to calm her racing heart as Colin held her hand. Images of more raced through her mind, including intimacy. She wanted to beat a fist against the side of her head to get that thought out of there.

Maybe it was the handholding, not to mention how he shifted in his seat. Every so often his thigh brushed hers, sending waves of awareness through her system. This beautiful, funny, sometimes a pain, but mostly good man was one of her best friends, and she couldn't help wishing for more.

Even if I didn't think about it, it was always there at the back of my mind.

Her throbbing toe was what finally pulled her thoughts away from Colin. She had an excuse to take her hand out of his to rub her foot.

"What is it?" he whispered.

"Shush. Nothing." She still hadn't replaced the stupid shoes, which were worthless. Why did she even wear them tonight? She didn't need to impress anyone.

He pressed his lips so close they brushed her ear. "I'll rub your feet later."

She stared at him wide-eyed, but he didn't notice. Her throat dried, and her pulse went nuts.

Don't think it, Keleeja.

Applause broke out, and she focused on the stage. The song ended, and the kids bowed then scrambled away as the curtains closed. Lights came up overhead, and Keleeja looked around.

"I think there's a break while they change into their costumes. Then we'll have a short play."

"Wow, I never knew kids' programs were so elaborate."

"It's not that serious. Trust me. But it *is* cute."

Tawney appeared in the aisle beside them. "Colin, you can buy snacks in the hall now."

Keleeja laughed. Was she invisible? No, over the last year or so, Tawney had grown less and less shy, and she loved Colin. Plus, Keleeja could read her mind. She wanted Colin to buy *her* snacks.

"Aren't you guys having a party after the program?" Keleeja took a moment to tuck Tawney's shirt into her skirt better. Her class played instruments during the program. Tawney was learning the violin.

"Yes, but I'm hungry now." She poked a lip out, and Keleeja rolled her eyes toward the ceiling.

Colin stood and took Tawney's hand. "Let's figure out what we want to buy. Think they have cookies?"

Her grin broke out. "Yeah!"

The long evening ended with Keleeja dropping off in the car. She couldn't keep her eyes open another second and dozed to the sounds of the girls doing the same in the back seat. Some time later, she felt herself being lifted and she startled awake.

"Colin, what are you doing?"

"Shh," he said gently and smiled.

Her heart did somersaults in her chest. This must be a dream, and she drifted off again. The next thing she knew, sunlight streamed through the window, and she sat bolt upright in her bed.

A peek out of the side of her eye showed the empty bed, and she let out a sigh of relief and disappointment.

Colin either carried her to her room and left her on the bed fully dressed, or she wandered there only half-awake. Either way, she missed him.

"Don't, Keleeja."

How could she see him in anything but a romantic light when they had such a great time the night before? They had hung out together all afternoon and evening, taking care of the girls together.

"But he wouldn't want that every day, so stop thinking about it." In the grand scheme of things, Colin could enjoy visiting because he could go home whenever he liked. He didn't have to commit to the exhausting task of having young girls ask him a million questions a day and whine his name through the bathroom door the second he sat down on the toilet.

She laughed as she climbed out of bed. No, it was better to keep him as a friend. At least he was in her life, and she was far less lonely with him around. In fact, the more she thought about it, the happier she grew. Whether it was Colin or Autumn, there was always someone there for her. They might not be conventional, but they were all a family.

"And that's more than enough."

The bell rang just as she finished cleaning up in the bathroom. She tried to remember what day it was. Oh yes, Saturday. No school, nothing planned except chores. Who would be stopping by at that time of the morning? Maybe it was a delivery. She better move before someone got a notion to answer the door.

After throwing on a robe, she hurried to the top of the stairs and then stopped cold. Colin stood in the doorway, talking to Daniel, who stood outside holding a tiny bundle in his arms. From the looks of it, Colin had opened the door from inside her house.

As the implications struck her, Daniel's gaze shifted from his friend up to her on the stairs in her robe with bare feet. His eyes widened and jaw grew slack. A greeting stuck in her throat, and Daniel didn't say anything either.

Colin grinned and stepped back. "Come on in, man. Make yourself comfortable."

Keleeja bit back a laugh. *That dummy. Trying to give wrong impressions.*

She continued down the stairs. "Oh, Colin. Did you stay over on the couch? I was dead to the world last night."

His eyes twinkled, and his lips twitched. "No, I slept upstairs. I'm hurt you don't remember."

Daniel's head swiveled back and forth between the two of them. "I'm sorry. Did I come at a bad time?"

"Would you stop, Colin?" She peeked under the blanket wrapped around the baby. "Let me see your son. I heard you had a boy."

Colin had kept her informed during Isabella's pregnancy. According to him, Isabella was ten times worse being pregnant because her hormones were all over the place. He'd wondered how Daniel kept his sanity and had taken to only talking to his friend on the phone or away from the house so he wouldn't have to deal with her. Keleeja had felt bad for Daniel.

Daniel's chest swelled as a proud papa. "This is Parker. He's two months old today."

Keleeja sucked in a breath at the sweet face. "Wow, he looks just like you. Same eyes, same lips. So cute."

Colin frowned. "Are you complimenting him or the baby?"

"Shush." She held her hands out. "Can I hold him?"

Daniel handed his son over, and Keleeja sat down, cuddling him close. She breathed him in then removed the blanket as the house was warm enough to keep him comfortable. The little bundle of joy wiggled in her arms, kicking his little feet, and drooling on his fist. Keleeja's heart ached a little.

Keleeja remembered the men and looked up. Both stared at her. "Oh, sorry, Daniel. Sit down. How've you been?"

Before he could answer, the troops rushed in, loud and energetic.

"Daniel!" They shouted and rushed him. He opened his arms wide for a hug from each.

Lara noticed Keleeja and wandered over. "A baby! Where did you get a baby, Lee?"

"I found it on the doorstep."

Lara's eyes rounded. She was still so easy.

Keleeja laughed. "I'm kidding. It's Daniel's son. Isn't he cute?"

"Yes." Lara leaned against her, wrapping an arm about her neck. She practically climbed on Keleeja's lap before Keleeja stopped her.

"Be careful, Lara. You don't want to hurt him."

"Are you keeping him?"

"No, he's just visiting."

"Okay." She relaxed.

Keleeja met Colin's gaze over Lara's head and mouthed, *"Jealous."*

He laughed and nodded.

"By the way…" Keleeja looked around. "Where's Tawney?"

"She's still in bed." Lola, after hugging Daniel, had moved to cling to Colin's side. Daniel noticed the attachment, but Keleeja couldn't read his expression.

"Still in bed? At this hour?"

The girls were always up before her, especially on the weekend.

Colin rose. "I'll check on her."

He left the room, and the triplets trailed behind him like baby ducks.

"Wow," Daniel commented. "They've really taken to him. Are you guys together?"

"Not really."

"Hm."

She eyed him, rocking his son gently. "What does 'hm' mean?"

"Well." He grinned, and she was struck anew at how handsome he was, even more so than Colin. "I stopped by because…uh…"

"What's up with you? Why are you so nervous? Wait, you didn't come here wanting me to babysit, did you?" She was only half-joking this time. For some reason, her heartrate kicked into high gear.

He chuckled and relaxed. "No. The truth is, I came to ask you out."

CHAPTER 26

I'm still sleeping. That must be what this is about. It's a dream.

Keleeja set plates all around the table. Colin sat at one end, and Daniel took up the other. Neither man seemed to care that she usually sat in one of those spots. No, they were too busy giving off vibes that demanded the other leave. How did she get in middle of this mess?

Of course, she could ask Daniel to go. She'd enjoyed meeting his son, cuddling the little one to her heart's content. Seeing Parker's daddy satisfied her curiosity about how he was doing, especially after he informed her that he had never gotten back with Isabella, even after he found out she was pregnant.

"And she's gotten better as a person," he had told her. "She puts Parker before her own needs."

"Wow."

"Yeah, I was surprised too. I thought it would be all

me, trying to give my son what he needs, but Isabella is a good mother."

"I'm glad for Parker's sake." She honestly was because she loved kids, and they deserved loving parents. It was hard to believe Isabella changed so much after giving birth. Keleeja knew nothing about the changes a woman went through during and after pregnancy, but she'd heard many times that a mother would give her life for her kids from the moment she knew she carried them.

"Are you going to say something about me asking you out?" he'd gone on to say.

Then Colin walked into the room, and the subject was dropped. From then on, sparks flew between the two men. Keleeja had come close to kicking them both out, but she had to consider Tawney.

While Daniel sat at one end of the table with his son in a carrier in front of him, Colin sat at the other end with a sick Tawney on his lap. Tawney didn't have to admit the truth to Keleeja. She could guess what happened. At the kids' party after the program, she must have eaten something with dairy. She knew better. Her teachers knew better, but Tawney could be stubborn. Now she had a stomachache.

"Feel like eating lunch, Tawn?" Colin rubbed her back.

She buried her flushed face into Colin's neck and mumbled, "No."

"Okay. Don't worry. The meds will kick in soon, and you'll be right as rain."

Daniel frowned at him. "Why are you acting like her father?"

"I'm concerned. She's not feeling well. *You* don't need to comment."

"Both of you, *quiet*," Keleeja growled. "There will be no arguing at the table or around the girls. *Period*. Am I clear?"

Both men muttered apologies.

"And for your information, Daniel, the girls love Colin. If he helps keep Tawney calm while she heals, I'm fine with it. Why would you have a problem with that?"

He held up his hands. "I don't. I'm sorry, and you're right. Tawney comes first."

Keleeja continued to bring in lunch with the triplets' help. Since it was Saturday, they didn't usually eat lunch at the table. Her rules were laxer on that day. But since they had a full house, Keleeja made an exception. None of the girls complained. They loved having visitors and liked to be in the thick of things.

The tension in the room bothered Keleeja. She wanted Colin there, but she worried too. Was she asking too much? Daniel's desire for a big family fit her big family better. Now that he had his son, he might be in the best frame of mind to accept her girls.

Her mind whirled as she tried to figure out what she wanted. And even if she did figure it out, was it possible? The decisions weren't all up to her.

She looked over at Colin as she sat down at the table. He was jealous of Daniel being there. She wondered if he'd heard Daniel when he said he wanted to ask her out. His jealousy didn't mean he wanted something more than friendship from her.

Ugh, this is so frustrating. I wish I could turn all these feelings off and just live!

"Tawney, baby, you want to sit by me or go back to bed?" Keleeja asked her.

Her little sister peeked out at her. Keleeja saw the desire to be nearer to her big sister, but the wish to stay with Colin won out. Bed was out of the question since she might miss something.

"Well," Keleeja moaned. "I guess I've been replaced."

Colin laughed. "Don't worry. It's just temporary. She'll be wrapped around your leg again soon."

Temporary, right.

After lunch, Keleeja returned to her weekly chores. She left Daniel and Colin in the living room, hopeful a fight wouldn't break out. With two loads of laundry done, she grabbed the basket with more to fold and headed back to the living room.

"I already beat you twice, man," Colin bragged. "Ready for one more?"

"You're on!" Daniel jabbed the controller to start a new round on the racing game. Colin brought the game over along with a couple others months ago and left it there, before he learned the girls didn't like that kind of game. Apparently, he and Daniel did.

Keleeja sighed in relief to see the two friends getting along. Even as she found a seat and started folding clothes, the tension from earlier didn't return. Colin and Daniel were back to normal with each other.

They played round after round, neither of them

paying her any mind. Even as they shouted, Parker slept through it all. Colin and Daniel were having a good time. They egged each other on, threatening jokingly. Keleeja had had enough.

"Just how long are you two going to take up space in my house playing games? The girls are cleaning their room, and I'm doing laundry. After that I have a million and one other things to do, including running errands. But don't let me get in the way of your fun."

Both men jumped to their feet. Colin shut the TV off, and Daniel apologized, his face reddening. "Sorry about that, Keleeja. It's been a while since I got to hang out with Colin."

Colin shrugged. "Every time I visited you, she was around."

Daniel frowned. "You know it wasn't like that. I had to make sure she was taking care of herself for the baby's sake. He means everything to me."

Guilt stirred in Keleeja's gut. They had been getting along before she ruined it. Colin slapped Daniel on the shoulder, grinning.

"I know, man, and I feel for you. It must have been a nightmare for six months."

Daniel flushed again. "Partly. I had the anticipation of seeing Parker."

Colin agreed. "Now, you're going to have a new anticipation."

"What's that?" Daniel looked confused.

"The fun of folding laundry."

Daniel drew back in horror, and Keleeja burst out

laughing. She jumped on Colin's suggestion and put both men to work.

"This will be good practice for you, Daniel." She handed over a few of the girls' tops. "For folding Parker's things."

"I've already had practice. He's two months old, and he stays with me almost as much as he stays with Isabella."

She eyed him. "You've been folding his clothes?"

"Well…" He coughed and muttered something she couldn't understand. What was up with men and folding clothes? Was it to be avoided like the plague? Or maybe it was just these two men and their issues.

Her cell rang, and she checked the screen to find that Autumn was calling. While Colin taught Daniel how to fold the pink unicorn top of all things, Keleeja stepped outside.

"Hey, girl. What's up?"

"Lee." Autumn's voice trembled.

Keleeja gasped. "What's wrong?"

"Nothing. I'm just excited. I finally feel like I can tell you."

"Tell me what?"

Autumn giggled like one of the girls, giving Keleeja a clue to what was coming. It had to be love. Nothing else could change a woman's temperament like that. Autumn wasn't the giggly type unless she was playing with Keleeja's little sisters.

"I've met someone, Lee. He's so great."

"Wow. I'm happy for you, sweetheart." Keleeja did feel happy for Autumn. Her friend had lamented being alone for years. Men weren't beating her door down to date her because of her body. But Keleeja had always known someone special was out there who would love her like she was and see the good woman she was inside. "Who is he? And when do I get to meet him?

"Tonight, if we can come over. I'll give you all the details. I'm ashamed to say I've been seeing him for two months without telling you. I just wanted—"

"You wanted to be sure. I'd give anything for a little of that, trust me."

"What about you?"

"What about me? I'm still single."

"You know what I mean. What about Colin?"

"I don't know."

"You love him."

"That doesn't sound like a question."

"It's not. You two have been as thick as thieves for months. It's obvious."

"It should be obvious that we're great friends. That's all. Autumn, he doesn't want to be burdened down with four daughters right off the bat. Who does? It's too much to overcome."

"In your mind. You haven't given him a chance."

"And I won't!" Tears filled Keleeja's eyes. "He means so much to me. I…"

She gasped and covered her mouth. Out of the blue, the truth came sharp and clear. Autumn was right. She hid it from herself, lied in her own head. She told herself it was friendship and even chanted it to keep herself from facing the truth. In one second, the mental barrier she built came crumbling down.

She thought about how Colin behaved with them when he came over. The memory came to mind, of Colin holding Tawney in his arms, comforting her when she was ill. His wonder at watching the girls perform, and even the way the girls looked to him as much as they looked to Keleeja struck her hard.

"No," she said with a sniff. "I can't change things. You don't understand."

Autumn's tone gentled. "You're scared. I understand that."

"No, I'm saying I *won't* try to change things because they need him. Even if it's just like this, it's going to be enough. Can you imagine me trying to push for more and him rejecting me? Then we get awkward, and he starts to pull away. It will break the girls' hearts. I can't risk that. I *won't*."

"What about your needs, Lee?"

"No," she insisted. "It hurts, but I'm putting them first—always. Plus there are really good times with him just like we are. It's not complete, but it's good when it's good."

"Okay."

Autumn didn't push the point, and Keleeja sighed in relief. She didn't want to argue, especially since it made no difference. Yes, she loved Colin, and as sweet as Daniel was, he couldn't compare. Her decision was final. Done deal.

"Look, bring your friend over for dinner tonight. I'll make something."

"Are you sure? I forgot it's Saturday, and you'll be

done in with all the cleaning. I won't put the burden of cooking dinner on you too."

"It's not a big deal. I'll make a pot of spaghetti with some garlic bread and a salad. That's both hardy and good, and I can throw it together in a heartbeat. I even have all the ingredients, so I don't need to go to the store."

"If you're sure."

"I am. Come."

"Okay. See you tonight."

Keleeja hung outside longer than necessary and leaned against the side of the house. After a moment, she wandered to the end of the drive. Visions of her and Colin as a family came to mind, and she shook. Tears filled her eyes, but she drove them away. What she said to Autumn was how it would be. No matter how much she loved him, she wouldn't push for more.

Daniel came to mind and his claim that he had come over to ask her out. Tempting as his suggestion was, just to avoid loneliness and because he was a great person, she would turn him down too. Same reason. Colin might leave.

"Lord, I've got it bad. It's a no-win situation."

One of the neighbors jogged along the opposite side of the road and waved to her. Keleeja waved back. The neighbor looked beyond her and waved again. Keleeja looked around to find Colin heading toward her. His face at her home was so familiar even the neighbors recognized him.

He reached her with a serious expression on his face, and her stomach knotted. "We need to talk."

"What about?"

"Daniel. He told me he came to ask you out."

She whirled away, turning her back on him, and rubbed her arms. At some point the temperature dropped by several degrees. "So?"

He gently turned her to face him. "It's time for some distinctions to be made."

"What are you talking about, Colin?"

He tipped her chin up, scowling down at her. "It's time for my best friend to understand that I'm not giving you or the girls up. Not for him, not for anybody!"

"**W**ha-ja-ja—" She sounded like an idiot, but whatever she intended to say refused to form on her tongue. Her brain tilted. She must not have understood him correctly. Maybe what he said didn't mean what she thought it did. She wanted him to explain himself, but she couldn't voice the question.

"Whaja?" He grinned. "Not sure what that means. Is it a foreign language?"

She smacked his arm. "You know good and well it's not. Stop playing, Colin. You caught me off guard. What are you talking about?"

"We'll always be friends," hung on her tongue, but she refused to say that. It would give him an easy out and her a way to protect herself from reading into his words. No way. Not this time. She chanted that mantra for months. If he was trying to say something special, let him come out with it. She wouldn't help.

"It's simple." He leaned back, folding his arms across

his big chest. "I'm saying I like what we have."

Her heart sank.

"I like coming over here, hanging out with you and the girls as often as you'll let me. If I had it my way, I would be here every day and every night."

Her breath caught in her chest. "You…I…" She took a minute to calm down. "Careful, nut. You'll be giving me ideas. You know how women are."

He stepped closer and ran his hands along her arms. "I *want* to give you ideas—fantasies really. Of you and me together. Not just as friends. But I don't want to presume you feel like I do. At the same time, I don't want Daniel coming over here and getting ahead of me."

"Oh." That's all she could say.

"I wanted to give us some more time together as friends. It hasn't been a full year since Sherrie died. I still love her, but I love you too. And I want time to see if what I feel for you is real and not just me looking for someone to take her place."

Her mouth fell open. "Colin, you can't say you love me in that off-handed way. And you definitely can't say it right after you say you love another woman!"

"I'm sorry. I'm screwing this up." He pushed both hands into his hair and turned away. "How do I say the right thing? I don't want to blow it."

He muttered to himself, searching for the right words. As far as she was concerned, he already did. He expressed his heart. She got it. Knowing he loved her felt good. Thinking he wasn't sure about that love hurt. But she understood.

"Alright," she told him.

He looked at her. "Alright, what?"

"You have all the time you need. I want time too. I have to be sure you aren't going to get sick of the girls and walk out. They love you, and it would kill me if at some point you couldn't take the noise and constant activity. Then you disappear."

"*They* love me. What about you?"

She hesitated. Admitting it opened her heart to being broken. This wasn't a prepared declaration between them. Circumstances rushed them into it.

"Do you think your friendship with Daniel will survive if we start dating?"

"You're avoiding my question."

"Stubborn!"

He grinned. "Scared?"

She rolled her eyes. "Fine, I love you, okay? Happy now?"

He drew her against his chest and brushed his lips over hers. Her head spun when he let go so fast.

"Wha—?"

"In case the girls are watching. They might think I only hugged you."

"A kiss isn't adult-rated, you know."

He laughed. "I know, but we don't want them to think we're a couple until we solidly are."

Her heart melted. He was always thinking about the girls and what was best for them. She didn't have to remind him. It made him father material, even if they were both hesitant.

She laid a hand over her eyes and rubbed them. "You're too much."

"Is that a positive too much or negative?"

She laughed. "Positive. I wish…"

"Yeah?"

He sounded hopeful. She peeked up at him, and her heart went crazy, beating wildly for him. He was so cute, so perfect, and they were great together. It felt like too much to hope for.

The day her mother walked out of their lives, she felt devastated, hopeless, like she would never find anyone. The chances of finding a good man were hard as it was. To add the complication of a big family right off the bat made the odds astronomical. Yet here he was.

"I wish we could be alone to explore this revelation between us."

He stared at her with a wonderous expression. She started to question the look, but he explained. "You're always so open. You speak your mind, but you're kind at the same time. It's funny. I saw that you're more special than she was, even when I hurt the worst."

She gasped.

"When I think about it, that's what saved me. Just… you being you, Keleeja."

He cupped her face, drawing close. She started to remind him about his resolve to keep the change in their relationship a secret from the girls for now. Then she junked the idea. Let him touch her. It felt amazing. Her body warmed and vibrated. She wanted a whole lot more.

"Keleeja," he breathed, studying her face. "So perfect."

"I'm not perfect."

"Perfect," he insisted. "On second thought, if this isn't real, what's real? What value does it have? You're who I want. I love you. Let me show you how much."

She could hardly draw a breath. "I love you."

"Marry me."

She shrieked in alarm and jerked out of his hold. "Whoa. We just talked about needing time and—"

"I know, but do you want to wait? I don't mean get married tomorrow. We could get engaged and draw out the planning."

"It would hurt more if everything fell apart in a month."

"Would it? If you're considering saying yes, would it hurt more if you did say yes and we stopped seeing each other?"

"I don't know." She stumbled, and he grabbed her elbow to lend her support. "I'm so scared I feel ill."

"That's not the response I wanted. I'm sorry. I'm impulsive. Pretend I didn't say anything."

"You changed your mind?"

"No."

He didn't elaborate, and his gaze seemed steady enough. She licked her lips. "You're not asking because you want beat Daniel to the punch, are you? I said I'll wait for you. I like Daniel, but he's not for me. I kept thinking more about you than him right from the beginning. Every time you two were together, I found myself looking at you instead of him."

"I like hearing that."

"So you don't have to rush because you're worried about my feelings for Daniel. Even when we were dating, I wanted to talk to you so bad. I missed you."

He dragged her into his arms and held her tight. She clutched his shirt and pressed her face into the hollow at the base of his neck. Breathing in his scent and feeling his warmth comforted her. She wanted to stay like this forever, but they needed to get inside. Who knew what the girls were up to.

"I'll try not to rush, but I want you to be my wife. I feel surer now that I've said it out loud. It might be knowing you feel the same about me that's giving me a boost. If you say yes, we'll dump every doubt before we tie the knot. Deal?"

"Deal."

They headed back inside the house. The high-pitched squeals and giggles let Keleeja know the girls were fine up in their room and that they didn't witness her and Colin's clinging to each other. She went to check on them anyway and found their room a mess.

"Girls, I thought you were cleaning up in here."

Lola popped to her feet, leaving dolls and their clothes scattered everywhere. "We did clean up. But then we started playing with our toys again."

"I didn't see it the three seconds it was clean."

Lola shrugged, like such was life, and Keleeja gave up the argument. After she left the girls, she headed downstairs to the living room where she'd left Daniel. He sat quietly rocking his son, staring at nothing.

"Where's Colin?" she wondered.

"Bathroom." He gazed at her a moment. "I'm disappointed."

"Huh?" Her stomach knotted, and she sat down.

"I'm disappointed that we can't be together."

She gulped. "You saw?"

"You and Colin outside? Yeah. Sorry, I spied. I guess I saw it coming. I'm the one who insisted our first date be at his house. It makes zero sense that I would do that."

"You were worried about him at the time."

"Yeah, and maybe fate played a part, putting us all into position." He sighed, giving off an air of sad resolution. "He kept talking about you whenever he called. I told myself it was just gratitude for you rescuing him when I couldn't be there. Seeing you two together showed me I was wrong. Colin loves you, and I see that love reflected when you look at him. I missed out in a big way. Still, if he's happy, that's everything to me."

"Thanks, Daniel. Right from day one I could see you were a good man."

"But not *your* man."

She smiled. "I'm sorry."

"Don't be. It's not like I fell in love and had my heart broken. I was hopeful. Anyway, it's a big deal to capture Colin's heart. Don't let him go."

"I won't. But…" She bit her lip. "Don't you go away either. If it's not too hard, stick around us, okay? Please? I know we can all come together like a family, and I don't want to leave you out."

"Thanks. That means a lot to me too."

CHAPTER 28

"Whoa, what?" Autumn shrieked.

Keleeja shushed her. "Keep your voice down."

Autumn grabbed her arm and squeezed it too hard. She jumped up and down, biting off another squeal. "Did you hear what you just said?"

"I said it. I should have heard it, silly." Keleeja laughed and removed her arm from her friend's vise hold.

"What happened in the few hours between our talk on the phone and me getting here? You didn't give me a clue that you were engaged!"

"I'm not exactly engaged. Well almost. Kind of. It's unofficial."

"Would you stop trying to take it back? Tell me everything."

Keleeja perked an ear up to listen to the noises in her house. The place was certainly lively, just the way she liked it. Daniel and Colin had taken to Autumn's boyfriend as soon as they met him. The three were competing in the racing game, shouting insults at each other.

Keleeja walked to the kitchen doorway. "Keep it PG in there."

The girls were upstairs playing something in the hallway. Keleeja heard them running back and forth. From the sound of it, they had dug out the bowling game she bought them last year. She hadn't seen them play with it since Christmas, and she'd been planning to give it away to charity. Good thing she didn't.

"Lord, it's noisy here." She returned to the stove to check on the water for the spaghetti noodles. A rolling boil had begun, so she dumped the pasta into the pot. Autumn busied herself at the island cutting three different cheeses into small cubes.

"That's the way you like it," Autumn said. "If it was too quiet, you'd worry."

"Only when it comes to the girls. That's when they're up to something. I'm scared Colin will get tired of it. He's a single man. He has a big family, but he's lived on his own for a long time. To go from silence to Grand Central Station is a big leap."

"Sounds to me like he wants to take that leap. Lee, you didn't dare to believe you could have someone because you're raising your sisters. You've found a great guy. Don't run away from it."

"I'm not. I'm just scared."

"Aren't we all?" Autumn paused in her cutting. "You've seen my man. Look at me. I'm fat. I worry some thin little princess is going to take him away. What is someone like him doing with me?"

Autumn's boyfriend seemed like a nice guy. Keleeja liked him as soon as she met him, but he was no catch in the looks department. Ordinary features, a tad bland, and super skinny. She doubted women were lining up to date him. What he lacked in looks and weight, he made up for in height. The guy had to be two times Autumn's squat height. That might be an exaggeration but not by much.

"And you're telling me not to worry?" Keleeja shook her head. "He's into you. I can see that."

Autumn grinned. "He is. But I'm human, you know?"

"Yeah."

They were silent a while as they continued to put dinner together. Keleeja popped the garlic bread into the oven when the spaghetti was almost done. The delicious smell of garlic and oregano filled the air. Her stomach growled.

The thumps on the second floor moved to the stairs and then the girls burst into the kitchen.

A chorus of small voices sounded off at the same time. "I'm hungry, Lee."

"I know. Wash your hands. We're about to sit down in a minute."

They scampered off to the downstairs half bath and were back in seconds. Keleeja looked them over, love filling her heart. She adored her sweet sisters and wanted herself and them to have Colin.

Questions swirled in her head along with doubts.

Would he stay? Was he really the one? Could they make it work long term? Fear choked her, more than she ever recalled in her life. Even when she realized her mother had abandoned them, she wasn't this afraid.

She'd been taking care of the girls since their birth. She knew the routines she had established. They had been closer to her than her mom from day one. But this thing with Colin was different, and it didn't depend on just her. He had a say.

"Girls, set the table, please." She sent them into the dining room and lowered her voice to speak with Autumn. "Remember the nights they cried for her?"

Autumn moaned. "Your mom? Yeah, but it didn't last long because you were like their mom all along."

"Yes, but it still hurt them. They may have emotional damage in their hearts. I can't imagine how it'll affect them when they grow up. I don't like thinking about it."

"They're happy, Lee. Look at them."

She peeked into the dining room to watch her little girls scampering around.

"No, I get to sit beside Colin this time," Lily was saying. "You did last time, Lola."

Lara raised her chin in a show or rare spirit. "Well, *I'm* sitting next to Daniel."

"You can't decide that for yourself," Lola complained.

Keleeja laughed.

Don't let them fight over boys when they're older!

"I see they're happy, even more so with the guys around. They absorbed them in like they were already a part of the family. That worries me, Autumn."

"Okay, worry."

"What?"

Autumn patted her shoulder. "Worry. I can't stop you. You can't stop it either. So feel it and live on. Keep having a good time with Colin. Marry him when you're ready and enjoy that too for however long it lasts. Then if he ever breaks your heart…after I break him, you can tell yourself, 'It was amazing while it lasted and at least I had that!'"

"You have a point. There's no sense holding back. For what? To be miserable? To worry? To keep second-guessing myself? Now that I think about, there are two possibilities here." She ticked them off on her fingers. "We continue as we are, as friends, and eventually he gets sick of all the noise and responsibility and walks away. My heart will be broken, and I'll have only spent that time longing for more with him."

"I get where you're going with this."

Keleeja nodded. "Yup. Or I jump in with both feet, have a good time as a couple with a lot of fun nights! A girl gets supper lonely, if you know what I mean."

"Yes, I do!"

They laughed together.

"Then if he goes, I can know that I had that much. 'Cause seriously I've been counting the years since the last time I had a boyfriend. This stinks!"

"It's a miracle we both have them at the same time."

"I know." Keleeja sighed. The logic made since to her, to have Colin fully in the way that she desired him. It didn't make her less afraid. She still felt like she might pass out just thinking about it, but the impulse he showed earlier bubbled up inside her.

She waited until after dinner and the girls were in bed. Daniel had gone with his son and so had Autumn and her boyfriend. She was alone with Colin, something she cherished. After taking a quick shower and joining him in the living room, she curled up next to him on the couch and leaned into his embrace.

They shared a few kisses, and she pressed her lips to his throat. The strong beat of his pulse vibrated against her mouth. She breathed deep, bringing in his unique scent that drove her senses wild.

His arms tightened around her. "I love you."

"I love you too. That's why…" She swallowed.

He drew back and tilted her chin higher so he could look into her eyes. A worried light came into his, and she knew he'd been thinking about her fears all day. Her mom had made a huge impact, not only on the kids but on her. At that moment, she realized half her terror came from feeling abandoned—even when her mom was still around.

"You think I'm perfect, Colin, but I'm not. Inside, I'm kind of damaged."

"Keleeja—"

She touched a finger to his lips. "But I'm strong too. And determined. *She's* not going to take anything else from me. So I have a proposal."

"I'm listening."

She had the feeling he thought she would suggest he move in, or they get engaged and give it more time. She couldn't wait to correct him on that notion.

"Marry me tomorrow."

His mouth fell open, and his beautiful silver eyes widened. *"What?"*

"Marry me tomorrow. No preparation, no planning. Let's just do it. Tomorrow, you become my husband and sort of like a daddy but really a big brother to the girls. What do you say?"

If she expected him to jump up and back away, stuttering that he needed to make sense of her suggestion, *he* corrected *her*.

"Yes! Let's do it. I would say today, but it's already too late, and the kids are in bed. Tomorrow, you become Mrs. Colin Voss."

A thrill of fear and excitement rocked her body.

He drew her onto his lap and nipped her earlobe. "But tonight, I'm going to practice being a perfect husband, who meets your every-single-expectation."

The End

ABOUT THE AUTHOR

Tressie Lockwood has always loved books, and she enjoys writing about heroines who are overcoming the trials of life. She writes straight from her heart, reaching out to those who find it hard to be completely themselves no matter what anyone else thinks. She hopes her readers enjoy her stories.

A Note From Tressie,

I would like to thank you for reading my book. If you enjoyed it, please take a moment to review it and to let a friend know about me. A good review can help an author reach more people, and others will take a chance like you did. Thank you for your help, and happy reading.

- Tress